The Golden Sword

(The Camelot Inheritance ~ Book 1)

~ When the past and present collide ~

Also available in The Camelot Inheritance series:

The Time Smugglers

Merlin's Vow

The Golden Sword

(The Camelot Inheritance ~ Book 1)

Rosie Morgan

There are more things under the heavens
than we can ever imagine.

The Golden Sword

ISBN: 978-1497402249

First published in paperback in 2014 by Liscarret Creations
This updated edition 2017

Both the characters and the events in this story are entirely fictional; however the setting is loosely based on the beautiful landscape of the county of Cornwall, Britain.

Illustrations by Rosie Morgan

Cover design by Katie Stewart, Magic Owl Design

To Dad
a.k.a.
Grandad Tom

Map of Bodmin Moor

to Pendrym

Table of Contents

Chapter 1

Hunted

Later, Arthur would wonder why he'd wished for a more interesting life. His had been fine as it was. School, skateboarding and hanging out with his friends should have been enough. But maybe it wasn't his wish that changed everything – maybe it would have happened anyway.

***

At the end of the street the mist swirled and shifted. A shape flew out of the cloud, circled once and settled on the gate post of a slightly shabby, terraced house.

Moments later a man appeared, wearing a long coat and a wide-brimmed hat. He strode purposefully along the street before coming to a halt outside the house where the bird waited.

If anyone had been there to see him they might have noticed the way that his dark eyes narrowed and his jaw clenched. Or they might have seen him quickly glance around before adjusting his hat, pulling the brim low over his face, and reaching into his coat pocket.

The stranger examined the house, taking in the scruffy paintwork and the rough path. He shook his head and muttered quietly to himself. The bird cawed and flew up to the roof and cawed again. The man watched the bird and then glanced towards one of the upstairs windows; he appeared to be considering his next move. Finally he nodded, took something out of his pocket and tossed it to the ground. Flashing a brief look at the same bedroom window, with its curtains still closed, he smiled. It wasn't a pleasant smile. The boy had no idea what was waiting for him.

Still smiling, the stranger turned and strode into the mist.

The bird cawed once, spread its wings and followed its master.

***

'I'm going to call Nick ... we'll probably head down to the Yard,' Arthur shouted towards the stairs. He shifted his skateboard and pushed his phone into his pocket.

There was a muffled 'Okay' followed by the inevitable question: 'Have you got your key?'

'Yeah ... don't worry!'

'Would I?' asked his mum, leaning over the banisters.

'Is there a day without a 'y' in it?' he said, then grinned and shot out of the door before she had time to come up with an answer.

It was a perfect day near the start of the summer holidays when endless, empty days lay ahead and all thoughts of school and homework could be banished for a few weeks. Arthur didn't mind school but this was much better. The sun had burnt away the early morning mist leaving uninterrupted blue sky, not a wisp of cloud remained to hint at how the morning had started.

Arthur skated down the hill away from his house, enjoying the smooth whirr of the skateboard's wheels on the pavement and the sun on his back. He was completely absorbed in the ride so didn't hear the crackle and the *woomph* as he whizzed past a narrow alley. A street cleaner appeared behind him and watched him skate down the gentle hill. Arthur cruised to the end of the street and the man stepped back into the shadows – and there was another *woomph*.

Pulling his phone out of his pocket, Arthur skated round the corner and called up a number. He smiled as he waited. It was obvious Nick wasn't up yet. His friend answered just before the message cut in.

'Nick! You said you were going to be out by now.'

'I nearly am,' his friend answered before yawning. 'Anyway, would I miss a day like this?'

Arthur grinned. 'Well, there have been times when the effort to get out of bed has been too much.'

'Not often!' Nick protested.

'Yeah ... whatever. Look, I'll see you in a minute. Just don't be long.' He pressed the button to end the call, cutting off Nick's protests, and slipped his phone back into his jeans pocket.

Coasting down the road, Arthur passed other groups of kids from school. He said 'Hi' to some as he sped by but he was fairly preoccupied with thinking about the weeks ahead. A lot of time would be spent skateboarding at the Yard with his friends, although they'd probably take the train to the beach as well. It was great being old enough to go down to the coast by themselves this year.

But he wasn't far from the Yard when these thoughts were interrupted. A dark bird swooped over him and cawed. Instinctively Arthur ducked and looked up ... and then looked around. Something was wrong.

He frowned. It felt as if something important had altered, but the shops and houses were just the same. The enticing smell of baking bread still drifted from the open door of the bakery, and the sign above the florist's shop continued to flash its 'Pippa's Petals' in that disgusting neon pink.

However, all the bird song had stopped; instead there was just a heavy silence. And this was the main road, it was usually packed with cars, buses and bikes, but now there wasn't a single vehicle in sight. Furthermore the sun, and the picture-book blue of the sky, was being replaced by slate-grey clouds and an ominous gloom.

Arthur was scanning the street again, doubting the evidence of his own eyes, when he saw that it wasn't completely empty. A man was standing not ten metres away, with a crow perched beside him on a low, red-brick wall.

At first glance the stranger seemed old, but as he looked more carefully Arthur decided that he couldn't be so sure of his age. He studied his clothes and wondered why anyone would choose to wear a long, black coat and a dark, wide-brimmed hat on a summer's day.

But perhaps the most disturbing thing about this man, apart from his companion and his clothes, were his eyes. They were expressionless and unblinking, and they were looking straight at him.

Arthur slowed, coming to a halt several metres away. He looked up and down the road but it was still deserted. Then he looked back to the stranger and it was as if the man had been waiting for Arthur's full attention because now, very slowly and deliberately, he raised one arm and pointed right at him. He frowned and narrowed his eyes as if he was taking aim, and appeared to be focusing all his energy in Arthur's direction.

The atmosphere shimmered and rippled, there was a *whoosh*, and Arthur felt as if he was being pulled through the air. The daylight disappeared and Arthur was standing on the summit of a moonlit hill, he had his arm outstretched and was holding something cold and metallic. Now he was raising it up and looking out over a sea of people.

He was vaguely aware of others standing beside him and that, although there must have been thousands gathered around the hill, there was absolute silence. Another *whoosh* and he was back on Station Road in Lyskeret, facing a stranger with a crow at his side.

He stumbled and caught himself. What on earth had happened! Nausea welled up; that familiar sensation of travel-sickness which dogged him whenever he was driven any distance. Except this time he hadn't been travelling in a car.

Arthur met the stranger's gaze and the man's concentration faltered. He looked up to the sky and then all around him. His hand trembled as he pointed towards the boy and his lips moved, but Arthur couldn't hear the words.

As Arthur stood transfixed, trying to register what had happened moments before, a single drop of rain fell. This wasn't particularly unusual, but what followed was quite out of the ordinary. Even in Cornwall.

Overhead the sky had continued to darken as more clouds had gathered and far off to the east there was the faintest rumble of thunder, and then the rain started in earnest.

At first there were only a few drops splattering and exploding on the dusty pavement, but within seconds the individual droplets had become a deluge. Waterfalls flowed off the roofs and on to the ground. Rivers of water streamed down the pavements and cascaded through the street. In seconds the stranger was drenched, soaked to the skin; but although his adversary was only metres away not a single raindrop had touched Arthur. He was completely dry.

He looked up, into the eye of the storm and the circle of blue sky directly above him while the rain continued to fall. And then a rainbow arched over his head, shimmering from red through to violet – the most intense colours he'd ever seen.

'What's going on?' he muttered.

But it seemed that he wasn't the only one to be taken by surprise. Judging from the way that the stranger was switching his gaze between the torrential rain and Arthur, this was not what he'd expected.

The man's face darkened, his frown deepened and he stood absolutely still. Arthur waited, wondering what else could possibly happen.

The stranger's jaw clenched and a pulse ticked in the side of his forehead. He fixed Arthur with an ice-cold look.

For a moment they stayed where they were, neither of them moving, but in the next instant a bolt of lightning lit the sky, thunder crashed overhead and immediately there was a shower of black feathers as the bird took to the skies. His master paused and the seconds ticked by until, finally, the dark-eyed stranger reached a decision. He glared at the rainbow and then, hunching his shoulders, flicked a final, burning glance towards Arthur before turning and vanishing down a flooded alley.

Invisible to Arthur, the street cleaner stood leaning on his broom and Watched.

He turned and spoke into the shadows behind him. 'So you have finally arrived, Servo! I expected you to be here before.'

The cleaner paused and turned again to look at Arthur. 'Look, this is the boy you have been summoned to Watch. I believe he is The One.'

The shadows exclaimed, 'This boy? Surely he is too young. He will never be able to lead others.'

'He is of the right age and family,' the cleaner said. He added, 'You should have arrived before and you would have been witness to all that happened. The Writer won't be pleased that you were late.'

'I can only Watch in one place, Viatoris!' the shadows replied sharply.

'Where have you been Watching that's so far from here?'

'My assignment is to Watch the boy in Egypt, Jacob's youngest son, the one called Joseph. He's more than three thousand years from here.'

The street cleaner shifted the broom to his other hand, 'Ah, Joseph the Dreamer? The one sold into slavery by his brothers?'

His companion nodded. 'The same.'

The street cleaner was thoughtful. 'But Joseph was a mere boy yet he was chosen.' He paused. 'You see? Age is no barrier to destiny.'

The two Watchers contemplated the boy before them.

'If he is The One then we can expect others to gather,' the cleaner stated. 'And if Brane and the crow are here then *she* will be near.'

At which point the other Watcher commanded, 'Quiet. Watch!' because the second the stranger had rounded the corner the rain had stopped, but now something else was happening.

Sitting on a low garden wall across the road from Arthur, was an enormous, green-eyed cat. As soon as Arthur noticed it, it began purring: a huge, base rumble.

Then it stretched and meowed and leapt down from the wall. Arthur stood, mesmerised, as the creature padded towards him because, incredibly, it appeared to be both growing bigger and changing the colour of its coat. The rich ginger colour was deepening to a dark, puma-like black and, with every step it took, it was growing.

Arthur's heart pounded. He couldn't move. But the moment the cat reached him it just rubbed against his legs, walked around him once, and disappeared up the same alley into which the stranger had retreated.

The cleaner lifted the broom into a cart and spoke quietly to his companion. 'So, Cathe is here too.'

There was a silence behind him.

The very faintest of whispers answered.

The street cleaner listened intently. 'I'll tell the Writer that you Watch in Egypt. She may summon you back, Servo; you may be needed here. We have already seen Brane and his crow, and now we have also seen Cathe. I think it is beginning.'

A tiny whisper of protest reached the listening cleaner.

He smiled. 'You can say that to the Writer yourself. Oh, and wear clothing suitable for Cornwall on your next visit. It's colder and wetter here than it is in Egypt!'

An exclamation mark floated across the years as the cleaner pulled his cart back into the shadows and disappeared.

***

For a while Arthur stood rooted to the spot.

The storm clouds had dissolved to be replaced by brilliant sunshine and blue skies. The water steamed and rose as the pavements dried. And little by little, as if he was waking from a dream, he became aware of people having to step around him and examining him curiously.

'Excuse me young man,' grumbled an elderly lady, 'your skating-board is in my way.'

'Sorry,' Arthur mumbled, before adding automatically, 'It's a skateboard.'

But throughout this exchange his thoughts were caught up with the moonlit hill, the empty street and the sudden storm. He looked down to his skateboard and then at his surroundings: traffic flowed up and down the main street, birds filled the air with their song, and people crowded the pavements. He swallowed. None of this made any sense.

He put a foot on the skateboard and pushed off, picking up speed in his anxiety to get to Nick's house – and safety. Then he noticed that the ground beyond the end of the street was dry.

Not a spot of rain had fallen there.

Chapter 2

Trapped

Arthur leant on the doorbell with his heart hammering in his chest.

Nick flung the door open and then saw Arthur. 'I thought I was meeting you at the Yard?'

Arthur nodded. 'You were.'

His friend frowned, puzzled, but when Arthur didn't say anything else he just shrugged and opened the door wider. 'Oh well, you'd better come in. I'm having breakfast; do you want any?' But without pausing to hear the reply he was on his way to the kitchen and to his primary interest: food.

Arthur followed him down the narrow hall and into the tiny room. A stack of papers filled one chair, and a pile of washing another. Arthur shoved his board under the table, found the only empty chair and sat down heavily.

He felt sick. Food was the last thing on his mind. He wanted the clock to be turned back to that moment when he'd stepped out of his house – when the sun had been shining and everything had seemed so ordinary.

He toyed with his keys, turning them over and over while he thought. He knew it would sound mad but he had to try to tell Nick about the man and the bird and the rest of it. He was glad Nick's mum was at work so he didn't have to pretend he was all right in front of her.

'Listen, something really weird happened just now ...'

'Yeah? Want some toast?'

'No ...' he paused while he tried to organise his thoughts. 'For starters, there was this strange guy ...'

But Nick was focused on his breakfast. 'Pass me the jam, mate. Sure you don't want any?'

Arthur shook his head. He tried again.

'Look, this guy ... well, somehow he cleared the street,' he started. 'And then there was this cat, it wasn't a normal cat ... and it changed ...'

Arthur's attempt at describing his experiences faded as he recognised the impossibility of trying to tell Nick what had happened without sounding totally mad. He watched his friend eating, all the time trying to still the thoughts buzzing through his brain.

Who was that guy and how had everyone vanished? And what about that cat?

As for finding himself on top of a moonlit hill – now that was beyond weird!

So it was just as well that he didn't look out of the window because the ginger cat had arrived. It was sitting on the wall of Nick's front garden – and it wasn't alone. A street cleaner was taking a particular interest in the pavement outside the gate.

Then a bird appeared, a very dark bird, and circled above them.

The street cleaner leant on his broom and Watched.

The bird flew lower, and the cleaner looked down the street at a dark-coated man hanging back in the shadow of a tall gate post. 'Ah, so that is the way you want to play this game,' he muttered to himself. 'But Cathe will not sit idly by and watch as I have to.'

The moment he'd uttered these words there was a flash of fur and teeth and the cat was leaping high into the air. There was a squawk, and a feather came spiralling down to land at the street cleaner's feet. The bird flew vertically upwards, only narrowly escaping the cat's claws, and back to the safety of its master. The cleaner's eyes met those of the bird's master and something unspoken passed between them. And then the man was ramming his hat down and snapping his fingers at his bird and turning away. The cleaner Watched Brane and the crow as they followed the road over the curve of the hill until they'd disappeared, and then he relaxed. A little.

Meanwhile the cat sat on the wall and washed itself. Wherever it washed, its fur would change from ginger to black and back again. And its paws were growing and shrinking. It was as if it hadn't quite decided whether to be a normal cat – or something else entirely.

The cleaner Watched the cat and smiled with satisfaction. He had done his job well. Then he turned and trundled his cart slowly along the road. The cat finished washing, settling at its original ginger colouring – and original size – then it leapt down from the wall and padded softly away.

Inside the house, blissfully unaware of the drama that had taken place, Arthur decided that he had to have another go at describing to Nick what had happened for the sake of his sanity. He'd burst if he kept it to himself.

There was one way guaranteed to capture his friend's attention: food deprivation. So Arthur leant across the table and swept the bread, butter and jam out of Nick's reach.

'Hey!' Nick exclaimed indignantly, clutching a piece of toast.

At last Arthur had his undivided attention. 'You've got to listen, Nick!'

He paused, wondering how best to describe his experiences, and decided to start at the beginning.

'You know I called you?'

Nick nodded, his mouth full.

'Well … just after that, the street went really quiet, and then there was this strange guy …'

'Yeah I know, you told me, but every town has its characters.'

'Yeah, but this guy wasn't just a bit odd, it was more than that.'

'I knew you should've eaten,' Nick said, cramming the last of the toast into his mouth.

'Listen to me!'

'Okay, okay, go on then,' Nick sighed.

At last Arthur was able to tell Nick about how the street had become deserted, and to talk about the stranger, but when he began to describe how he'd stayed dry in the storm his friend stopped him.

'Look, I can see this guy might have been a bit – different, and there might have been some heavy rain, but we are in Cornwall, rain isn't exactly a novelty! C'mon, get your board and let's get outside.'

'Yeah but it was much more than that …'

But it was clear that Nick had heard enough; he was already on his way out.

Arthur muttered, 'Great, thanks,' and was almost out of the door when he noticed a book wedged between a pot of dried-up flowers and an old teapot on the windowsill.

He was intrigued. Nick didn't like reading and, furthermore, this book was no ordinary book. Fascinated, he reached across the debris of Nick's breakfast and picked it up and examined it. The edges of the pages were finished in gold and the cover was deep red leather, richly decorated with images of knights, castles and animals. A pair of knights jousted in one corner, a unicorn stood in another, while along one of the borders a dragon appeared to be flying over a castle. He'd never seen anything like this in Nick's house. He glanced out of the window to see his friend making his way down the path to the front gate. Arthur traced the gold lettering embossed on the cover. He'd just flicked it open, ready to inspect it in more detail, when he was summoned by an impatient shout from his friend.

'Come on!' Nick was shouting at him.

Arthur glanced back to the book. There was something about it that drew him to it, something familiar, but his friend was already out of the gate. Reluctantly, he laid the book on the table and followed Nick, pulling the door shut behind him.

As he sped down the path, the pages of the book lifted and turned. They came to rest at an illustration – of a moonlit hill, with a boy standing on the summit, surrounded by an immense crowd.

***

Nick took the lead, skating with perfect control, weaving in and out of the pedestrians.

He was easy to spot with his bright, blond hair, and he'd grown quite tall in recent months, so Arthur was able to track his progress along the crowded pavements. He was leading the way towards the Yard near the centre of town which had been converted into a skate park by the town council. It had half-pipes to skate on and benches which were usually jammed full.

When they arrived at the Yard, Arthur's head was still full of the stranger and the moonlit night.

'*And not just a man, more of a … Crow Man,*' he thought to himself. But the rational side of his brain still searched for a reasonable explanation; anything to take the strangeness out of the morning. However, as soon as they arrived at the Yard, both he and Nick realised that something out of the ordinary was going on because the Yard was completely deserted. And it was *never* deserted in the holidays.

'That's odd,' Nick said.

'Yeah, right, I've never seen it empty!'

Arthur took in the vacant benches and the unused half-pipes. This had to be more than a coincidence.

'Maybe we should go.'

'No, let's make the most of it!' Nick said, brushing away any worries, and launched himself at the pipes. The Yard echoed to the thumps and bumps of the board taking off and landing. Nick practised some flips and tricks but Arthur couldn't trust himself to skate. Instead he just perched on the back of a bench and watched Nick and wondered.

A flash of lightning coursed through the sky, closely followed by a rumble of thunder. Arthur looked up as another lightning bolt lit up the Yard and, swinging off the bench, sprinted for the shelter as a single, black feather floated down to land on the seat where he'd been sitting just a few moments before. And then, from outside the Yard, there was a piercing shriek followed by a yelp and a small, enthusiastic animal rushed in through the gate to land panting at Nick's feet.

'Mug Shot come here! Hey guys, did you see that lightning?'

The dog was followed by a girl wearing jeans almost worn through at the knees, and trainers which were definitely not bought to be a fashion statement. Her hair was dark, nearly black, and hung straight down her back. It was Tamar, the third of the trio – she'd practically grown up with Nick and Arthur. They'd started school on the same day and they still spent most of their spare time together.

'Hi guys. Mug Shot come *here*! Stop dribbling over Nick's nice, new trainers.'

'He's not dribbling over them, he's drowning them,' Nick retorted. '*And* you made me crash, look at my elbow,' he said, holding it up for inspection. But if he was expecting sympathy he didn't get it.

She just glanced at his injury and flicked her hair back. 'It was probably the lightning that made you fall.' Then grabbing the dog's lead, she did the whole, 'Bad dog – must walk to heel' thing, while her pet panted and grinned at her.

Eventually the dog rolled over and lay on its back with its feet in the air; a small, round, brown and white barrel. Tamar giggled and, shrugging, gave up.

'So what have you two been doing?'

'Dodging lightning!' Arthur said.

'Drying my trainers,' grumbled Nick.

'Yeah, right!' Tamar shot back.

It only ever took a couple of minutes for Nick and Tamar to be in the thick of a heated disagreement. It didn't need to be about anything at all, but if one of them took a point of view it could be almost guaranteed that the other would choose the opposite.

So before the exchange could disintegrate into the usual argument, Arthur interrupted them. 'We've been skating, Nick's been doing some really cool flips …'

'Hey, that's not the total truth is it? *I've* been skating and you've just been sitting on that bench and gazing into the distance.'

'Look … it's been a strange morning.'

'Yeah, like it's rained!' Nick retorted.

Arthur flashed a look at Nick. Sometimes he seemed to go out of his way to be difficult.

Ignoring Nick, he turned to Tamar, 'What've you been doing?'

A dark shadow flitted over the Yard. Arthur looked up and caught a glimpse of a crow. He shivered. It felt as though an icy finger had run its nail all the way down his spine.

'Nothing much, so I thought I'd come here. I was making Mug Shot walk to heel, he'd done really well ...'

'Gold star, Mug Shot!' Arthur said enthusiastically, rubbing the dog's head. He was determined to shake off the feeling that something major was building.

'Then we were coming up to the alley, you know the one with Steve's Garage in it? So I decided to let Mug Shot off his lead and see how well he walked without it ...'

'Needs more practice,' Nick interrupted.

Tamar threw a withering look in his direction and, sighing dramatically, continued. 'Well, this guy stepped right out in front of me. Honestly, I nearly walked straight into him.'

'What did he look like?' Arthur asked, casting a look up at the darkening sky. Storm clouds were stacking up again.

'He was really peculiar – he didn't say sorry or anything.' She paused and shuddered. 'Yeah, and he just stood there and looked at me. Boy! You should have seen his eyes; they were straight out of a horror movie. He looked like a huge bird or something.'

She stopped and frowned and thought. Then her face cleared. 'I know what he was like ... he was like a giant crow!'

Tamar looked at Arthur. 'Are you okay?' she asked, because her friend's brown eyes had widened under his dark fringe as an intense stillness filled the Yard. And anything Arthur was about to say was forgotten. A shadow fell across them and slowly each one of them looked up. Standing at the Yard's entrance was the stranger. The three of them sat on the ground, held by those cold, black eyes.

They were trapped.

Chapter 3

The custodians

No traffic noise filtered in from the street, the birds stopped singing and even Mug Shot was quiet. Instead of a fresh summer breeze, a scent of mustiness and decay filled the Yard.

Then two things happened: Tamar's phone rang, which wasn't unusual, and the cats arrived, which was.

At first just one or two appeared, strolling into the Yard with their tails held high. They took no notice of the large bird perched on the wall to the side of the Yard – or of the dog – instead they meandered towards the centre of the space. However, after a few minutes their numbers began to swell until whole groups of cats were climbing and leaping on to the red-brick wall that enclosed the Yard, and flowing through the entrance to the park.

They were of every imaginable colour and size: from delicate long-haired Persians and blue-eyed Siamese, to sturdy tom-cats with torn ears. Silently they prowled towards the three friends, sitting motionless on the Yard's floor as the furry tide streamed around them.

Tamar's phone continued to ring but eventually the ringing stopped and then there was just silence – apart from the quiet padding of many paws. The three friends glanced at one another and then mutely shuffled closer together. Tamar reached down to Mug Shot who was having his own canine crisis. This many cats in one place was more than any dog should have to endure.

It was becoming clear that the animals were organising themselves in some way and that there was one definite leader: a majestic ginger-and-white tom with penetrating, green eyes. It was the same animal that Arthur had encountered that morning.

The tom stood directly in front of them, facing out towards the Crow Man. The other cats fanned out on either side of their leader creating a perfect semi-circle. Their intention was clear. They had arrived to protect Arthur and his friends from whatever the stranger had been plotting. Their purpose was also becoming obvious to the Crow Man.

Throughout this exhibition of feline solidarity he had stood, unblinking and unmoving, but it was as if he was only now beginning to realise the strength of the opposition.

He took a step forward but the cats instantly arched their backs.

He took another step but was met by a wall of hisses and spits.

The Crow Man's eyes locked onto Arthur. Seconds stretched out and joined up into minutes with the cats poised, ready to leap. Arthur's heart drummed, waiting for the man's next move. A single leaf drifted down from an overhanging branch, a bee buzzed above their heads and an emerald-green caterpillar inched towards the shelter of the wall, but nothing else moved.

Suddenly their antagonist came to a decision. Glancing at the cats, he motioned to the bird and it flew to his side. He fixed Arthur with those ice-cold eyes. That look said it all. This was unfinished business, they would meet again, and next time Arthur wouldn't be so lucky. Finally, with a swirl of his long, dark coat, the Crow Man disappeared through the Yard's entrance.

For a while the animals remained where they were, with their hackles raised and tails bristling, concentrating on the space where the stranger had been standing and ready to spring if he reappeared. It was many minutes before they started to relax – and then the withdrawal began.

Before they left, each cat would glance towards their ginger-and-white chief and then, as silently as they'd arrived, they departed. A furry river surging over the boundary wall and through the Yard's entrance.

Tamar and the boys sat and watched the cats' departure until the only one left was their leader. He prowled towards them with a deep, rumbling purr and rubbed against their legs. Then he too turned and sprang onto the wall before disappearing as noiselessly as he'd arrived. At that moment the silence was once again shattered by Tamar's phone.

Slowly they dragged their eyes away from the wall, and the space left by the cat, and looked at each other. Nobody said a word. For a while Tamar didn't try to answer her phone but eventually she reached into her bag.

Her hand was trembling but she succeeded in keeping her voice steady. 'Hi Wenna. Yeah I'm fine ... What? No, I'm down at the Yard with Arthur and Nick. I've brought Mug Shot too – extra training. Yes, the boys will look after me, don't worry! I'll see you later.'

She smiled shakily at the others. 'Sisters! It was Wenna. She's always worrying, or nagging. Sometimes she does my head in!'

Neither of the boys made a comment. They just sat and looked at the place where the Crow Man had been. Finally Nick broke the silence with a half-hearted attempt at humour.

'Well, at least I've had the honour of meeting the guy too. I was beginning to feel left out.'

'Some honour!' Tamar exclaimed.

'And you know what? I never liked cats but I think I've changed my mind,' he continued. 'Wonder what it's all about?'

He turned to Arthur. 'Could we go back to your place?'

Arthur nodded.

'Great.' He looked thoughtful but all he said was, 'Have you still got some of those chocolate-chip cookies?'

'You and your stomach,' Tamar snapped. 'Unbelievable! We've just met the weirdest guy ever and then been surrounded by an army of cats and you're thinking about food!'

'Oh come on, let Uncle Nick have a little, tiny smile.' Even now Nick couldn't resist trying to wind Tamar up.

'Leave it, Nick,' Arthur said. 'Come on Tamar, Mug Shot looks like he'd enjoy a biscuit. One cat's normally enough for him; he'll need counselling after that lot.'

'Don't know about Mug Shot needing help,' Tamar replied. 'I could do with some.'

Nick leant over and put his arm around Tamar's shoulders. 'I'll be your counsellor Tamar – I'd be dead good.'

'Yeah, right.' But despite herself she started to grin. The thought of Nick counselling anyone was mind-blowing. 'Don't call me; I'll call you!'

Nick tried an offended look but somehow it lacked sincerity and, without any further discussion, they gathered their boards and bags. Arthur looked at the sky. Once again the storm clouds had disappeared, traded for a deep summer blue. The weather was unusually changeable.

Tamar caught Mug Shot's lead and they made their way over to the entrance of the Yard. As they approached it they slowed down and Nick looked around the corner. He didn't notice anything out of the ordinary, just a street cleaner talking to himself.

Arthur glanced down. Something luminous had caught his eye. He picked it up and looked at it, but it was only a piece of stone embedded with fragments of quartz. He turned it over. He was fairly sure that it was the same sort that used to be dug out of the old quarry up on the moor. Arthur remembered that he'd collected some when his class had gone there on a field trip; they were probably still in a dusty box somewhere in his room.

Nick looked back to the others. 'Come on. It's all clear.'

Arthur dropped the stone into his pocket and let his skateboard fall to the ground then, giving it a push, he skated after his friends. Mug Shot raced ahead, trailing Tamar in his wake.

'So much for walking to heel,' Nick said. 'Hey, look I'm sorry mate.'

'What for?'

'Not believing you, or taking you seriously this morning, whatever.'

This was a pretty rare event. Nick hardly ever apologised for anything. If things had been more normal Arthur would have made the most of it but, right now, he couldn't care less. 'S'okay, forget it.'

After a while Nick asked, 'What do you think he wants?'

'Who? The old guy?'

'Yeah, course. I wasn't thinking of the President of America! D'you reckon he's interested in us?'

'Can't think why he would be. I mean, we're only kids, what's interesting about us?' Arthur said, desperately trying to convince himself.

'Yeah, and I reckon it was just a convention of cats!' Nick added with a touch of sarcasm.

He looked at Arthur and, seeing the anxiety written on his face, decided to change the subject. 'Come on, let's catch Tamar and the dog.'

'Okay, race you!' Arthur was determined to shrug off the sensation of something sinister closing in. It felt as if the whole order of things was being shaken up.

Chapter 4

Invaded

They ran down Castle Close and up the front path to Arthur's house, negotiating their way past the dustbin and a rusty wheelbarrow.

As they burst through the door Arthur shouted, 'Hi!' but no one answered.

His room was at the top of the house overlooking the street. From his window he could see above the roofs of the houses facing his, to the moors and silhouettes of the old mine buildings on the hills. They pounded up the stairs pushing each other out of the way, but for once Arthur got there first, with Nick and Tamar close on his heels and Mug Shot an enthusiastic fourth.

Arthur flung the door open and leapt across the room landing heavily on his bed, the others collapsed on the floor among piles of clothes and magazines. His room wasn't very big so every space was used. He had shelves bending under stacks of books and boxes, and a desk crammed with dirty mugs and plates leaving just enough room for his laptop. For a few minutes they all lay where they'd landed, gasping for breath, while Mug Shot wheezed at Tamar's feet.

After a bit Tamar said, 'Hey Arthur, I like the new screen saver.'

He looked over to the screen blinking at them from the desk. Swooping across it was a large black bird, possibly a crow, and in the background was something that looked like the hilt of a sword.

Arthur frowned. 'That's not my screen saver.'

As the words left his mouth Arthur felt, rather than saw, Nick and Tamar staring at him.

'So how did it get there then?' Nick asked.

It felt as if the temperature in the room had dropped. Their eyes were drawn back to the computer screen and to the bird silently plunging and diving across it.

'If it wasn't you, then who *did* do it?' asked Tamar, as they sat hypnotised by the rise and fall of the bird on the screen.

'I don't know. It can't have been Dad, he hates computers, and Mum's just learning – she hardly knows how to turn it on!'

'P'raps your dad's been taking lessons,' Nick suggested.

'No way – you've heard how he goes on about them!'

Arthur was really shaken. He was the only one in his family who was into computers so someone else must have been in his room. Someone from outside his family. Sunlight filtered through the dusty window, a siren wailed in the distance, and on the garden wall a cat yawned and stretched.

Nick raised his eyebrows at Tamar.

She nibbled her nails, trying to come up with a solution, while Mug Shot concentrated on chewing one of Arthur's old trainers.

Then Tamar's face cleared. 'I know! Why not go and find your mum and ask her who's been here? I bet she'll be able to tell us who did it.' And straightaway Mug Shot was being separated from the trainer and dragged back down the stairs.

Arthur forced his eyes away from the screen.

Nick shrugged, 'Come on, mate. I bet there's a simple answer.' He hauled himself up, thrust his hands into his pockets and wandered down the stairs after Tamar. Pictures flickered in Arthur's head – of the man, the crow and the cat. There wasn't going to be a simple answer.

Nick and Arthur ambled into the kitchen to find Tamar reading a note that had been left on the table.

She looked up. 'This is crazy.'

Arthur groaned, 'Not something else!'

She held the paper out. 'You'd better read this then.'

As he read the scribbled note his heart sank. It was from his mum telling him stuff about food and that she'd be back later, but the bit that grabbed his attention was the part about hoping he had his key. She'd added, 'Of course you'll have it – otherwise you won't be reading this!'

Arthur shoved the paper at Nick and thought out loud. 'We came straight in ... so maybe she forgot to lock the door.'

However, even as he was saying this, another part of his brain was busy with something he'd just noticed. On the floor, small but unmistakable, was a piece of stone identical to the piece he'd picked up earlier. Reaching deep into his pocket, he pulled out the stone from the Yard and held them side by side, comparing them, but there was absolutely no doubt.

The other two were watching him.

'What's up now?' Nick asked.

Arthur put the pieces down on the table. 'I didn't think it was important but maybe I was wrong.'

'What *are* you talking about?' Tamar asked.

'I saw this other stone back at the Yard and picked it up 'cause it caught my eye. I suppose I was sort of thinking that it could be something important and, look, they're the same sort.'

'Are you sure?' asked Nick.

'Yeah, definitely, I've got a load more in my room.'

'Well, maybe it's one of yours then,' Tamar suggested.

'No, it can't be. I haven't bothered with them for ages … I'm not even sure where they are.'

They were silent, until Tamar voiced what they were all thinking. 'The screen saver and the stone, he must have been here before us then.'

It was a blunt statement and they all knew who Tamar meant by 'he'.

She added, 'This is getting really bizarre.'

'Yeah,' Nick agreed. 'And, by the look of the guy, I'd say that he's seriously unhinged.'

'You've got to tell someone about him Arthur,' Tamar said.

Nick nodded, for once in agreement with Tamar.

'Yeah, it's okay guys,' Arthur replied. 'I'll talk to Mum when she gets in.'

'Good!' Tamar said.

Arthur looked at his friends. Nick was leaning back against the cupboards with his arms folded, while Tamar stood beside him with Mug Shot sitting obediently at her feet. They were a force to be reckoned with when they were on the same side.

'Thought you were hungry Nick,' he said, trying to distract them. He'd decided what to do and it didn't need more discussion.

His friend roused himself, 'I am … yeah.'

'Well there are biscuits in the usual place – help yourself,' Arthur offered.

They wandered into the front room and switched on the television.

A game show filled the screen with an enthusiastic audience and an animated host, but nothing could take their minds off all that had happened. Nick sprawled across the sofa while Tamar arranged herself in the armchair and cuddled Mug Shot. Arthur looked at them and wished he had a dog or cat or even a gerbil to take his mind off things.

He was miles away, contemplating the Crow Man, when Mug Shot suddenly sat up with his ears pricked as footsteps crunched up the gravel path to the front of the house. An intense stilllness settled on them. They heard the handle turn. Then the door creaked open and at last Mrs Penhaligon's voice called out.

'I'm ho-ome.'

Arthur realised he'd been holding his breath, wondering who, or what, might come through the door.

'Hiya Mum, in here.'

She poked her head around the door. 'Oh, you're all here, that's nice.'

Then she noticed Mug Shot on Tamar's lap. 'Ah, Mug Shot, who's a lovely boy den? Come to Auntie Chrissie.'

Mug Shot sprang off Tamar's lap to land at Mrs Penhaligon's feet and gaze up at her adoringly. It would have been touching if only he weren't quite so ugly.

'Mum …'

'Who's a bootiful doggy den? Mug Shot is, aren't you?'

'Mum, did you lock the door before you went out?'

'Of course I did. Aw, Mug Shot loves his Auntie Chrissie doesn't he?'

By now Mug Shot was lying on his back, all four short legs in the air trying hard to look as 'bootiful' as Mrs Penhaligon had convinced him he was.

'Is there any way you could have forgotten to lock it?'

Something in the tone of Arthur's voice registered with his mum and, glancing at him, she sat down on the arm of a chair and stroked Mug Shot.

'Okay, let me think,' she stopped and thought. 'Yes, I did lock it because I remember checking it.'

Nick, Tamar and Arthur exchanged looks but said nothing.

'Why? Is it important?'

'You could say that,' Nick responded.

'Why, what's happened?'

Tamar cut in, 'Nothing much – yet.'

Arthur's mum was looking thoroughly confused so he took over. He told her about their morning, although he left out quite a lot of what had happened to him, then both Tamar and Nick joined in, but not one of them mentioned the army of cats. They knew that most people would understand the threat of a strange man, but they also knew that the other events might be beyond an adult's comprehension.

However, it wasn't long before Arthur became aware that they'd lost his mum's attention. She was gazing out of the window while automatically continuing to stroke the dog. For a moment her hand froze as she peered through the glass, then she relaxed.

Turning back to Arthur she said, 'Sorry, for a moment I thought there were hundreds of cats out there, but there's only one or two. Strange though ...'

Her voice trailed away as her eyes were drawn back to the window.

Nick craned his head. He could definitely see more than a couple but he said nothing – just looked at the other two and nodded very slightly while he wondered how it was possible that the majority of the cats had become invisible to Arthur's mum.

'Sorry,' Mrs Penhaligon said again, turning away from the window. 'Where were you up to?'

Tamar swiftly summed up the rest of their experiences. 'And when we got back here your door wasn't locked and someone had changed Arthur's screen saver.'

'Do you mean that you think someone broke in?'

'Yeah, suppose that's what we mean,' Nick said thoughtfully. They hadn't put it into words before.

'But if somebody *did* break in,' Arthur's mum said, obviously doubting their story, 'it could have been anybody.' She continued, 'It didn't have to be the stranger you'd met.'

Arthur considered her point. 'Yeah, I suppose it could have been someone else ... but I don't think other people tend to carry these stones about with them. It's a pretty individual trait.'

'Is anything missing?' Mrs Penhaligon asked, still unconvinced.

'Haven't looked, but nothing obvious seems to be gone,' Arthur admitted.

Examining the sitting room, her eyes fell on the coffee table. 'Look, my purse is still here, no ordinary thief would have left that behind!'

'I know Mum, but this guy's not ordinary.'

She was quiet while she considered what she'd been told, weighing up the lack of any solid evidence of a break-in against Arthur's very real anxiety.

In the road outside, the cats had congregated on the pavement. A street cleaner leant against a tall gate post, blending with the shadows, while a crow glided above the crowd of cats before flying to the end of the road. But even if she had looked, Mrs Penhaligon wouldn't have seen any of this. It wasn't meant for her.

After a few moments she sighed, 'I bet the police will think I'm mad – especially as nothing's missing, but I'll give them a call. We ought to let them know about this man because, even if he didn't get in here, he sounds a bit odd. I'll phone them in a minute but first I'm going to have a strong cup of tea!'

Having made her decision, she gave Mug Shot a quick rub and went out to put the kettle on: Mrs Penhaligon's answer to any and every crisis.

'There were loads of cats out there you know,' Nick said, under his breath.

'I know,' Arthur agreed quietly. ' I saw them … it's odd that Mum couldn't.'

'I wonder what it's all about?' Tamar said.

'Search me,' Nick said, glancing at his watch. 'Hey, I've got to go. Can you give us a call and let us know what the police say?'

'Yeah course,' Arthur replied, 'although to be honest I'm hoping that there'll be nothing else to tell you.'

'Yeah, right!' Nick agreed before turning to Tamar, 'Want me to walk you home?'

Tamar's face displayed a mix of emotions, flitting between amazement and relief – although she'd probably have denied that.

'Yeah, actually I wouldn't mind the company,' she said, just a little too casually.

'Cool,' Nick said. 'See you later, Arthur.'

Arthur watched his friends make their way down the

road. Mug Shot was taking the lead with Tamar vainly trying to make him walk to heel, while Nick lazily skated along beside her. It all looked so normal, apart from an unusual number of cats lining the way, but he was beginning to wonder whether anything would ever be completely normal again.

He was about to go back inside when a movement caught his eye. He looked across the road to the house facing his. He had a feeling he was being watched but he couldn't see anyone. They had a new neighbour living there; he wasn't sure what had happened to the previous occupant although his parents probably knew. He hadn't seen her properly, just caught a glimpse of her entering her house as he was leaving his. Now he began to wonder why that was always the case.

Arthur glanced at the top window. It was empty, but he felt sure that there had been someone there a few seconds before; but maybe he was being paranoid after the events of the morning.

He looked back down the road. Nick and Tamar had disappeared from view and the cats were gradually dispersing, just as they had that morning at the Yard.

Arthur took himself up to his room, sat on the edge of his bed and looked around at his territory with its posters, mounds of crumpled clothes and stacks of books littering the floor. This was his space and someone had invaded it.

He slipped the stones out of his pocket, slanting them to catch the light, and wondered at their significance.

'*Why me* ?' he thought. '*I don't get it*.'

In the window of the house opposite, a curtain was pulled back and a face surveyed the street. In the road below, a figure emerged from the shadow of the gate post and the two exchanged glances. The street cleaner tilted his head as if he was listening to something, or someone, and nodded. He picked up a broom, balanced it on the cart and trundled down the street, losing definition and fading as he walked.

Together, he and the cart disappeared.

Chapter 5

Challenged

That evening there was serious discussion in the Penhaligon household. Arthur's dad had arrived home from work, ready to drop down in front of the television, only to be called into the kitchen as soon as he walked through the front door.

Mr Penhaligon was a big, reliable sort of man. The sort of person people turn to in a crisis. Nothing much ever ruffled him and, as they sat around the table, Arthur began to relax for the first time since that morning.

He was in the middle of telling his parents about the Crow Man, while carefully avoiding the subjects of massed cats or weird hill-top experiences. (His instincts told him that there were some things best left unsaid.) He'd covered the implied stalking, the probable break-in and altered screen saver and had moved on to describing the stranger. His father looked concerned, but didn't interrupt him.

Arthur sipped his tea and swallowed. 'You should have seen his eyes Dad – they were black … it was like he could see right through me.'

He faltered, because it felt as though the more he talked about the Crow Man – his winter coat, the broad-brimmed hat and coal-black eyes – the more the light in the kitchen dimmed and the warm air chilled.

His mum shivered and pulled her cardigan around her shoulders. Then a wind sprang up and rain began to fall in huge, heavy drops.

'Look at that weather!' Mr Penhaligon exclaimed. 'Where did that come from?'

As they looked out the rain became torrential, lashing the windows, rattling them as if something was trying to get in, until the kitchen window finally gave up and burst open, slamming back on its hinges. The rain swept in. Immediately Arthur's parents sprang up – but he didn't move. He was certain that he'd glimpsed a figure seconds before his dad had looked out of the window.

Then, as suddenly as it had begun, the rain stopped. The storm had succeeded in damaging the window catch and depositing puddles on the kitchen floor; so it was quite some time before the window was secured and the water had been mopped up, and by then Arthur felt unable to continue. It felt like the more he discussed the Crow Man, the stronger his adversary became.

In the silence that followed, Mr Penhaligon leant back in his chair and stroked his beard thoughtfully. 'You know the police will want a description of this guy, don't you?'

'Yeah, I know,' Arthur said, but inwardly he was beginning to doubt the power of the police in the face of the Crow Man. He'd been defeated today but Arthur felt that it could only be a matter of time before he succeeded in whatever he was trying to do.

He shoved his chair back, that fleeting figure imprinted on his brain. 'I think I'll give Nick and Tamar a ring to let them know what's happening.'

'Actually,' his dad said, 'you're looking whacked out. I think it's time you hit the sack. We'll phone them.'

For once Arthur didn't argue. Even though it was still early he was overtaken by exhaustion.

'Okay, but make sure you lock up properly won't you?'

Arthur glanced around. He thought he'd seen another brief movement outside the kitchen window.

His parents looked at one another and his dad raised his eyebrows. 'Okay, I'll check everything. And I'll make sure to put the bolt across the door.' He rested his hand briefly but reassuringly on Arthur's shoulder.

Arthur climbed the stairs. He was so tired he almost had to pull himself up, but a distant memory was refusing to be overlooked. He pushed his door open and stood in the middle of his bedroom. All he really wanted was to sleep, but something important niggled; so he closed his eyes and concentrated.

He frowned and tried to block the background noises: his parents talking, the low murmur of the television, the outside sounds of a summer's evening. And then his eyes flicked open.

'Of course!'

Dragging his chair towards his shelves, Arthur clambered onto the seat and reached up to the top shelf. He ran his fingers through the dust until he felt the smooth sides of a wooden box.

'Yes!'

He pulled it towards him, climbed down and pushed a pile of magazines out of the way. Kneeling on the floor he placed the box in front of him and the memories came flooding back. He saw a pair of weather-beaten hands holding the box out to him and heard the whispered words, 'Now boy, take care of this. It's for you.'

Slowly, Arthur prised it open and lifted the lid and was

immediately assailed by scents he'd long forgotten but would always link with his great-uncle: dried cloves and lavender. Lance's tastes had been unusual, but he'd always insisted on scattering a few of each among his clothes. Arthur peeled back a soft cloth bearing his great-uncle's initials, L.P. – Lance Penhaligon, and sure enough grains of faded lavender and a couple of cloves fell out of the cloth and onto his rug.

Arthur picked them up and was suddenly overwhelmed by the loss of a man he'd barely known. He could have only been about three when he last saw Great-Uncle Lance. He gulped back the tears threatening to engulf him. A shadow flickered in the corner, the smallest of movements, and just for a moment Arthur had the sense that he wasn't alone and wouldn't have been at all surprised to hear Lance's voice.

He shook his head, 'I'm losing it,' he murmured to himself, and returned to unpacking the box.

Cradled in the protective cloth was a carving of a knight seated on a horse while victoriously brandishing a sword. Of course; how could he have forgotten it?

The model was carved from the same stone that he'd found at the Yard; holding it up to the light it shone and glittered and, strangely, it felt warm. There was a word inscribed in the base but the writing was so elaborate that all he could make out was the initial 'B' and something that looked like a 'v' in the middle. It was probably a name but he had no idea what it could be.

He sighed, pulled himself to his feet and stood gazing out of the window as he idly traced the shape of the carving. He felt certain that this statue had something to do with the day's events, but he couldn't imagine what.

The storm had disappeared as quickly as it had arrived and the sun was beginning to set over the hills on the edge of the moors. He could see the silhouettes of mine buildings etched against the rose-red of the sky, and stone walls marking the edges of ancient fields. Birds circled, swept upwards by the currents of warm air, but they only brought back to him all that had happened and he decided it was time to sleep.

Despite all his experiences Arthur had no trouble sleeping and was soon unconscious; but his sleep was disturbed, dogged by dreams of being chased by dark, cloaked shadows. In one of the dreams he was escaping a faceless form – which was when he began to drift back into consciousness; his back was sweaty, his hair was wet and his T-shirt was sticking to him.

Arthur lay in the inky darkness wondering what could have woken him, when he heard measured footsteps walking along the path, away from the house, and saw a winged shadow flitting across his ceiling.

Curiosity overcoming his mounting fear, Arthur slid out of bed, crawled over the floor to the window and edged his way up until his eyes were just above the windowsill. His stomach lurched as he took in the scene on the street below him.

There, bathed in the glow from the streetlight, was the unmistakable figure of the Crow Man.

He wasn't looking at the house - he was looking towards the moors - but as Arthur watched it was as if the Crow Man became aware of him. He didn't attempt to move out of the light or to slip away, instead he slowly turned around and looked straight at Arthur, pinning him to the spot. It was just as before. There was no hint of emotion, only that coldly calculating stare. Slowly he reached into his coat pocket and took something out, all the time keeping his eyes locked onto Arthur. Turning the object between his fingers, he glanced at what he was holding and then back to the window. The meaning was clear. In the Crow Man's mind there was a link between the object and Arthur. Finally he threw it to the ground and tossed a look towards the window. It was a challenge.

Their eyes met and he raised his hand to the brim of his hat, mockingly saluting Arthur, and turned away. With his collar up and his coat swirling, he walked along the road and out of view.

For a while Arthur knelt by the window with his chin resting on his arms and gazed at the empty pool of light. His street looked peaceful, unchanged, as if nothing momentous had taken place.

In the house opposite, unseen because of the darkened room, a woman monitored the Crow Man's progress. She frowned and picked up a pen. Words hurried across the page, materialising before the pen reached them in their haste to be Written.

Chapter 6

The trail

A sound in his room woke Arthur.

He opened his eyes to see sunlight streaming in and realised that against all his best intentions he'd fallen asleep. He lay still, trying to work out where the music was coming from before focusing on his phone.

'Hi Nick,' he yawned, 'bit early for you isn't it?'

'Couldn't sleep. Thought you'd be up by now.'

'Would be usually – but I had a bit of an odd night,' Arthur replied.

'I'm not surprised after yesterday ...'

'No, that wasn't it,' he started.

'Why? Has something else happened?'

'Well ...' He stopped; he'd just caught sight of the stones on his windowsill and remembered that something had been left in the road for him.

'Look, can I call you later?'

'Okay, but don't leave it too long. And any more weirdness I want to know about it.'

'Yeah, course.'

Arthur levered himself out of his crumpled bed, padded across his room and looked outside. It was another perfect summer's day, but Arthur barely noticed the weather because something was glinting at the base of the streetlight.

Quickly casting around, he managed to find some relatively clean jeans and a T-shirt and pulled them on. He had to find out if his suspicions were right. As an afterthought he shoved the stones he'd found into his pocket and headed downstairs.

The scent of frying bacon floated upstairs, his family's customary start to a Saturday, accompanied by the sound of his dad whistling through his teeth. John Penhaligon was in the hall with the front door open, examining the exterior paint work. He'd painted it a couple of weeks previously, a rare event in this house, so no one could blame him for wanting to inspect his handiwork.

Arthur was nearly at the bottom of the stairs when his dad stopped whistling and began scrutinising the door more closely. He frowned and studied the area around the lock.

Rocking back on his heels, he called out, 'Come and look at this, Chrissie.'

A second later Arthur's mum came out of the kitchen wiping her hands. 'What? Oh that – it's a door.'

For once John Penhaligon didn't rise to the joke. 'Yes, but look at these marks. Did you make them?'

'Would I dare? It's more than my life's worth!'

Mr Penhaligon looked up and saw Arthur. 'Mornin' son. You don't know how this happened do you?'

'What is it?'

'There are lots of deep scratches in the wood. Look, they're all around the lock. They definitely weren't there yesterday.'

His voice trailed away and he slowly raised his eyes, meeting Arthur's, and then looked across to his wife.

The clock ticked, filling the silence. Eventually Arthur's dad said, 'Looks like your visitor has been trying to get in.'

Arthur paused, torn over whether to tell his parents about the Crow Man's nocturnal visit. He didn't want them to get too wound up and become super-protective. But eventually he decided that they should know about at least some of it.

'Yeah, he came back last night.'

'What, the man from yesterday?' his mum asked.

'Yeah,' Arthur continued, determined to play it down as much as possible. 'I heard some noises and then I heard footsteps. When I looked out of the window he was there, standing under the streetlight.' He stopped, that was enough information. No one needed to know any more.

Mrs Penhaligon looked worried. 'Why on earth didn't you wake us up?' But before he had time to answer she was already on to the next thought. 'And why's he so interested in this house?'

'Search me,' Arthur replied. 'Maybe he thinks we've got pots of money.'

She glanced around the battered hallway. 'That's not likely, is it?'

'Mmm, probably not.'

John Penhaligon stood up slowly, looking troubled; but Arthur, watching his dad's face, saw the worry turn into a decision. Then his dad reached for the phone, 'I'm going to give the police a call and ask them to come round this morning. I don't want to have to wait in all day. The sooner this guy is found, the better.'

Arthur said nothing, just nodded, although in his heart he doubted whether they'd be able to do anything.

He sat quietly in the kitchen listening to his dad speaking to the police on the phone. He was desperate to get outside to examine whatever had been left on the pavement, but he didn't want anyone else to know about the Crow Man's unspoken challenge.

He buttered some toast while he turned the events over in his mind. Whichever way he looked at it, he was at the centre of all that had happened. Arthur sat back and, preoccupied with his thoughts, took the stones out of his pocket and rolled them around the table before picking up the brightest one. He held it for a split second before dropping it as if it was red-hot. It wasn't hot, it was freezing cold; cold enough to feel like a burn.

'Ouch!' He shook his hand. 'How ...?'

But at that second his dad finished his conversation and put the phone down only for it to ring straightaway.

'Hello? Yes Tamar, he's right here. What's up with your mobile? Thought you didn't know how to use a normal phone!'

He chuckled at Tamar's reply and poked his head round the door. 'It's Tamar for you; apparently the old-fashioned ways of communication can come in useful sometimes!'

Arthur hurriedly swept the stones into his pocket, taking care not to hold them too tightly.

As soon as he picked up the phone Tamar started talking. 'Hi, are you okay? Nick said you sounded a bit strange this morning.'

'Yeah, I'm fine, just had a bit of a surprise that's all,' he said examining his hand. He actually had red marks on his fingers. 'I'll tell you later. What about you? You're not usually up this time on a Saturday.'

'Well, Nick said it could wait but I wanted to tell you as soon as I could. There were cats everywhere on our walk home yesterday!'

She continued with hardly a pause. 'It was exactly like it was at the Yard; they were sitting on the walls, under cars, in the gardens ...'

'I thought so. I watched you go down the road.' Glancing over to his mum, Arthur didn't add any more.

'Yeah, and then we noticed that they'd get up when we'd gone past them and leave. It was like they were making sure we got home safely. They were so ... so organised.'

'Cool,' Arthur said, but their conversation was brought to a halt by a police car crawling up the road towards their house.

His mum looked out of the window. 'That's quick! What did you say to them John?'

His dad looked sheepish. 'I may have laid it on a bit thick.'

Rolling her eyes, his mum sighed and said to Arthur, 'I think you'd better call Tamar back later.'

Arthur was secretly relieved to be able to leave the conversation there. 'Listen Tamar, I've got to go 'cause the police are here.'

'Police? Already?'

'Yeah, well ...' Arthur trailed off not wanting to go into details of the night's events.

'Okay, but remember to let me and Nick know if anything happens.'

'Yeah, course. See you.'

He felt a bit guilty that he hadn't brought either Tamar or Nick up to speed on all that had happened, but he couldn't face it right now – and his fingers still hurt.

***

As the policeman was being ushered into the house, Arthur could almost feel the curious stares from behind the curtains of the other houses in Castle Close.

'Suppose it's good to give them something to talk about,' he muttered to himself, then he realised that he'd have to wait to inspect the souvenir left by the Crow Man. He glanced up to the window opposite but as far as he could see there wasn't anybody there.

'So you're Arthur,' the policeman said, taking out his notebook. 'Not many of those around nowadays.'

'Ah well, Arthur's name is all down to his Great-Uncle Lance,' his dad began. 'He was a lovely old guy but he got himself so worked up about what we should call him, didn't he Chrissie?'

His mum smiled, agreeing. 'Yes, there was no way we were going to be allowed to call him anything else!'

Arthur squirmed. The number of times he'd had to sit through his parents telling this story; he knew it off by heart. He thrust his aching hand into his armpit.

'I mean, it isn't even a family name!' Arthur's dad continued.

At this point the policeman interrupted. 'That's very interesting Mr Penhaligon, but I think we ought to get on.'

Arthur silently agreed, but looking at the officer he seriously doubted that he'd be any sort of threat to the Crow Man. He felt sure that this was going to be a waste of time.

As Arthur started recalling the events of the past twenty-four hours he felt as though he was listening to himself from far away, disconnected from everyone else in the room. It was almost as if he was watching himself from somewhere far off, like in a balloon floating high in the sky, a fine thread the only thing keeping him from floating away. For an instant he had a bird's eye view of Cornwall

– even as far as the islands at Cornwall's toe – before his father's voice cut in, drawing him back to earth.

'I'd like you to see something,' he was saying to the policeman. 'I think it relates to what Arthur's told you.'

He led the policeman out to inspect the front door while Arthur tried to gather his thoughts. That had been really weird. Perhaps he hadn't slept enough the night before and maybe he'd just dropped off for a minute. He hoped that was the explanation anyway.

There were low voices and when they came back PC Coleman was looking grim. He sat down at the table.

'I'm going to speak to your friends Arthur, but I'll put out an alert describing your visitor straight away. Now don't you worry, in a small town like this someone as unusual as your 'Crow Man' will soon be noticed.'

''Scuse me a moment,' he said, and took out his radio. He tried switching it on but at first nothing happened. 'That's odd! It was working this morning.'

He adjusted the controls, turning dials, until at last a faint buzz filled the room. The radio crackled and then a voice wove through the interference talking about a boy and stones – and Arthur was sure he heard a sword mentioned. Then the voice faded and, for a few seconds, the buzzing continued until even that stopped, leaving them in silence.

The policeman looked uncomfortable. 'Sorry folks, that's never happened before. I'll have to wait till I'm at the station to put a call out, but I'll do it as soon as I get back.'

He stood up, signalling the end to their meeting, and made his way back to his car. Arthur stood back wrapped up in his own thoughts. Mr Penhaligon nudged him as the curtains at Mrs Trevithick's house fell back into place, 'Reckon it'll be all over town by this afternoon. He doesn't need to put out an alert. Just tell our neighbours!'

John Penhaligon was doing his best to be jolly, but it was a forced jollity. He kept glancing at Arthur, and there was a question in his looks. He was a shrewd man.

'Yeah, right,' Arthur agreed, ignoring his dad's unspoken questions while he considered the voice on the radio.

***

He waited until his mum and dad had gone indoors (his dad was getting too suspicious), before wandering nonchalantly, his hands in his pockets, towards the object waiting for him at the base of the lamppost.

It was a stone. The same sort that he'd found at the Yard.

Arthur picked it up cautiously but this one was at a normal temperature. Then he noticed that there were more at regular intervals all the way along the road. He wondered how far they went, and casually ambled along his street.

The trail didn't stop at the end of his street but led out to the main road. Not into town, but up towards the moors. Arthur shivered and turned back for home.

***

Later that morning, the street cleaner pushed his cart along Castle Close until he was outside Arthur's house. Then he turned and looked at the house opposite. A face appeared in the bedroom window. The cleaner nodded and watched as the observer placed a pair of round glasses on the end of her nose, picked up a pen and started to write.

Chapter 7

An ally

Arthur had a plan but he knew he couldn't tell anyone else. The sooner he could get on with it the better; however, he hadn't bargained for his parents deciding that it would be good for him to be taken out for the day. The moment that PC Dave Coleman had left he'd found himself being organised and consulted on what he'd like to do. He was too distracted to put up any sort of resistance. He knew that his parents were trying to take his mind off things, so in the end he agreed to go karting but all day he kept thinking about the Crow Man and the challenges he might have to face.

Nothing could dispel the feeling of some impending ordeal coming his way – something that he wasn't going to be able to avoid. And he was determined to meet it head on.

***

As John Penhaligon drove them towards Castle Close at the end of the day, a bolt of lightning shot out of the darkening sky.

'Would you look at that!' Arthur's dad exclaimed. 'We've got our very own storm.'

Blue-black clouds hung low, threatening rain, and as they drove up the street, thunder rumbled and pulses of white light joined the earth to the sky.

'I've never seen anything like it!' Arthur's mum said. 'It's almost centred over our house.'

Arthur looked up and down the road as his parents walked up the path to the scarred front door. There was no sign of the Crow Man but once again cats lined the road.

'Hi again,' he murmured to the large ginger tom sitting on his gatepost. 'So, you've been standing guard, hey?'

The cat stood and stretched; it was an enormous creature. This time it was at eye level with Arthur and he had the uncanny feeling that it understood everything he said.

'It's all going to be up to me isn't it? I'm the one this is all aimed at … I wonder if you'll be around to help.'

The cat started to purr.

'I'll take that as a "yes" then.'

It gave a single, deep 'meow' in reply and leapt off the wall, rubbed Arthur's legs and sauntered away. Interestingly neither of his parents seemed to notice the cats; perhaps they weren't meant to be able to see them. Maybe, as before, they were for his eyes only. The pace of events was definitely speeding up but Arthur had already decided that he was going to take control. He was going to make the next move.

***

Early the next morning he phoned Nick and Tamar. They were keen to get together to compare notes on their interviews with PC Coleman.

'And you can tell us all about your mysterious night-time visitor as well,' Nick suggested.

'Yeah, it was interesting!' Arthur said, ignoring the implied criticism that he hadn't told his friends about it first.

Casually he added, 'How 'bout getting out of town for a bit – fancy going to the moors?'

'Yeah, okay. We can't take our skateboards there though.'

'I know, but do you honestly want to go to the Yard?'

'Good point,' Nick said grudgingly.

'What, you mean you'll cope with a day away from your board!' Tamar exclaimed when Arthur put his idea to her. 'I didn't know you could manage that.'

'Wouldn't normally,' he said, rolling the stones around on his windowsill, checking their heat. 'But I don't want to go to the Yard today. Not after everything else.'

There was silence at the other end of the phone before she said, 'Oh, okay then. Mug Shot will be happy but it's not really my idea of an exciting day out.'

'Yeah, but doing something ordinary – even dull – will be fine with me right now,' Arthur said.

'Okay, I'll meet you guys at the bus stop in about half an hour,' Tamar agreed.

***

They chatted as they waited together at the bus stop. They had their phones, at their parents' insistence, and enough food between them for a small army. Or at least for Nick.

'Well, are you going to tell us about your visitor?' Tamar asked.

'Yeah, but let's wait till we're on the bus,' Arthur said.

They heard the old bus coming up the road long before they saw it. There was another person waiting, a lady of indeterminate age with long grey hair tied back in a plait and carrying a basket.

Tamar took control, putting her hand out to stop the bus, and the ancient machine shuddered to a halt and its door swung open. They all clambered on with Tamar engaging the driver in a long conversation about Mug Shot and where he was allowed to sit.

While they were waiting, Arthur became acutely aware of the grey-haired lady who'd sat herself at the back of the bus – and of her scrutiny. He was curious. She looked as if she was permanently enjoying a private joke. Meeting his gaze she smiled, and in that instant it felt as if she knew everything about him. Then she shifted and looked out of the window and Arthur found himself being drawn back into conversation with Tamar and Nick.

Tamar had finally settled Mug Shot at her feet. 'Sit down, daft dog!' she was saying, stroking him in an effort to calm him down. He wagged his tail enthusiastically; he was already having fun.

Nick had started on the chocolate biscuits. 'Well, are you going to tell us all about it, Arthur?'

'Only when you've given me one of those and when you've both told me what P.C. Dave asked you,' Arthur replied.

As the bus rattled up the lanes they exchanged notes on their interviews with 'Dynamic Dave', as Tamar insisted on calling him.

Their route took them up the road towards the moor; past high, Cornish-stone hedges, through picture-book villages and over a cattle grid, before finally bursting out into wide open spaces. But they were too focused on their conversation to watch the passing scenery, or to notice a single, dark bird flying above the little green bus.

Eventually Tamar turned to Arthur and said, 'Right, come on then, tell us about your special visitor.'

And even though it was sunny and warm Arthur

couldn't suppress a shiver. The thought of the attempt to break into his house and the further sighting of the Crow Man had unsettled him more than he'd realised. As he told his story the other two sat riveted in their seats. Unusually he had their complete attention – even Mug Shot sat quietly.

Then once again he experienced that feeling of being detached, of being far away, as he described the Crow Man's night-time visit. And just like before, he was brought back down to earth by somebody cutting in and asking a question.

'Where were they exactly?' Tamar asked. Her eyes had become bigger and bigger throughout Arthur's account.

'Er, where were what?' Arthur responded, glancing towards the other passenger who was watching him intently.

'You know – the stones that the Crow Man dropped,' she said impatiently.

Catching Arthur's eye, the elderly lady sent him a calm smile before turning away and tilting her head to look up at the bird high in the sky above them.

'Um, well, they started at the base of the streetlight, you know, where he'd been standing ...' he began, distracted.

'What d'you mean ... "started"?' Nick asked.

'Well, there were more.'

'And where were they?' Tamar prompted him.

'They sort of led away.'

'Wow! D'you mean like a trail?'

'Yeah.'

Nick encouraged him. 'Well, and what direction did they go in, or did they just stop?'

Arthur looked at the other two and swallowed. 'No, they led in a definite direction.'

At this point Tamar's whole attitude changed. Her brow furrowed. She'd been fiddling with her phone but her fingers froze and her eyes narrowed. 'And I think I've worked out what direction they went in and why we're out here.'

She continued talking, her fury barely controlled. 'You mean to say that you've brought us, your best friends, out here to get even closer to that crazy guy.'

She stood up now, working herself into a frenzy.

'Are you off your head, Arthur Penhaligon? I can *not* believe that you'd put us in this position. If our parents knew they'd be furious. You'd probably be grounded for the rest of the holiday and it'd serve you right.'

She held her phone in her hand ready to tap in a number.

Meanwhile Nick, who'd just been sitting quietly, said thoughtfully, 'Sit down, Tamar. Don't phone anyone yet.'

He said this with such authority – and unusual seriousness – that Tamar actually did as he suggested and reluctantly sat down. Surprised by his reaction, she stole a furtive look at him, although she still looked ready to explode. Glancing towards the back of the bus, Tamar noticed that the lady sitting there was looking at her. More astonishing though was the way she directed a serene smile in her direction and immediately Tamar felt herself calm right down. Then the woman, still smiling slightly, redirected her gaze out of the window at the passing scenery and the now empty sky.

Nick continued, talking now to Arthur. 'So do you think there's a link between the Crow Man, the stones and up here somewhere?'

Arthur nodded. He felt truly miserable.

Everything that Tamar had said was right, and it was made even worse because he'd brought them out here on false pretences. He hadn't exactly lied to them but he hadn't been up-front with them either. He sat mutely, head bowed, picking at the stitching on his bag.

Nick's voice broke into his thoughts. 'Where exactly do you think the stones come from? There's a lot of moor!'

'The quarry, I think,' Arthur mumbled.

'D'you know for certain?'

'Not for certain, no, but I'm fairly sure,' Arthur replied, unable to meet anyone's eyes.

They sat in silence, enveloped in their thoughts. From time to time Tamar would glare at Arthur but he just sat miserably looking out of the window, wishing he was anywhere but here.

The bus slowed and shuddered to a halt. 'We're here kids,' the bus driver called out. 'Have a good day and stay safe.'

They disembarked, momentarily distracted by rearranging themselves and their bags, while Mug Shot strained at his lead. He was ready even if no one else was. Then Arthur became aware of the other passenger standing beside him.

Swinging her basket over her arm the woman looked at him and said, 'You're not to worry now, it'll all work out – in time.'

Then she smiled, her eyes crinkling, and turned and walked down the road with her gaze once more focused on the wide, moorland skies.

Chapter 8

The chase

Arthur watched the woman as she disappeared around a bend in the road. He turned to the others wondering what they'd made of the exchange, but they were still engrossed in sorting themselves out. Nick was rearranging his backpack and Tamar was attempting to organise her dog because, in his excitement, Mug Shot had wound his lead tightly around her legs.

She looked down at him tugging impatiently, and muttered, 'Out with two mad boys and a mad dog. Great.'

Arthur stood silently. He was acutely aware of what he'd done and couldn't think of anything to say to make it better.

It was Nick who eventually broke the silence. 'Okay then guys, we're up here now. So what d'you want to do?'

'Ask Brain of the Century, not me!' Tamar snapped, irritably wrapping Mug Shot's lead around her wrist.

Nick looked thoughtful. 'Seems to me that now we're here we might as well go up to the quarry.' He unwrapped a chocolate and shoved it into his mouth. 'It could give us some ideas.'

'What! Like how to get captured by a mad man with staring eyes? Fantastic. Why not? Life is just too boring anyway!'

'Look Tamar, we've got our phones, it's a sunny day and there are loads of other people up here; I'm sure we'll be okay. Besides, what else do you suggest?'

Arthur glanced at his friends but said nothing.

Tamar looked like thunder. She glowered at Nick and didn't even bother to look at Arthur, but eventually she said, 'Oh okay, but if we see anything odd – anything at all – we'll phone straight away.'

'Deal,' Nick agreed and looked at Arthur who merely nodded.

Tamar untangled the tightening lead from around her legs and Mug Shot joyfully took off – a four-legged missile, hauling his owner ahead of the boys.

'I shan't remind her that we should stay together,' Nick commented, grinning.

Arthur watched Tamar being towed away from them and said, 'Look mate, it's my turn to say sorry. I should never have involved you two. I could have easily come up here by myself.'

'Yeah whatever,' Nick shrugged. 'What was behind all this anyway – fed up with being the victim?'

Arthur looked at him, startled that he'd read his thoughts so accurately. 'Well yeah, that – and this was the only positive thing I could think of doing.'

'Okay, and what exactly are you hoping to find?'

'I don't know – in fact I've no idea,' Arthur replied despondently.

'Yeah well, nice day for a walk anyway,' Nick said. 'Look, I'll catch up with Tamar and do the peace-talk thing. Give me a couple of minutes and then join us.'

Left alone with his thoughts Arthur looked around at the hills rippling into the blue distance. Much of the land was wild but some had been tamed and turned into a patchwork of fields separated by ancient stone walls. Here and there long-deserted mine chimneys rose up, grim silhouettes against the blue sky. To the side of the stony track a herd of shaggy-coated, long-horned cattle were surveying him watchfully, while above him a dark shape circled, slowly sweeping lower.

He trudged along the path, his hands in his pockets and deep in thought, when he noticed an exceptionally tall and upright figure striding towards him, a crook in one hand and a dog at his heel.

The stranger nodded imperceptibly at Arthur. 'Out for a walk with your friends?'

Arthur nodded back, his phone in his hand.

The man chuckled. 'No talkin' to strangers, eh?' Then his face changed, becoming serious, and his blue eyes became even more piercing. He looked up at the sky, then at the bird, which had flown ahead of Nick and Tamar.

'Fair enough, but weather'll be closin' in soon, I reckon.' Looking Arthur straight in the eye, he added, 'Probably be for the best if you and your friends don't go too far.'

'We're only going to the quarry.'

'The quarry, eh?'

'Yes,' Arthur replied, wondering why the man was so interested in where they were going. He was feeling more and more uncomfortable.

The stranger looked as it he was about to say more but instead he said, 'Well, take care now – and watch the weather.'

Then he touched his cap and strode off, whistling softly to his dog.

Arthur was puzzled. He looked up at the cloudless, blue sky and then back at the stranger, but he'd disappeared. He decided it would be better if he caught up with Nick and Tamar and jogged up the winding track, trying to ignore his mounting unease. Their goal was just ahead of them, around the next bend in the path.

They approached the entrance to the quarry. It was surprisingly narrow and felt more menacing than on the day of the school trip. Arthur glanced at Nick and Tamar and saw that they each had their phones in their hands. The walls of the quarry loomed up high and forbidding, and craggy rocks jutted out, blotting out the sun.

'Got your stones, Arthur?' Nick asked.

Arthur already had them in his hand and passed some of them to Nick. He was in no doubt that this was where they'd come from – furthermore, they were cooling down again.

'Yeah, definitely from here,' Nick said, holding them up against the rock wall. 'Wow, they're really cold!'

'I know,' Arthur said, distracted. 'They do that sometimes.'

'Do you reckon he's some sort of collector?' Tamar asked.

'Who?' Nick asked, examining the stones curiously.

'The Crow Man of course!'

'Dunno,' replied Nick. 'Some people have unusual hobbies. What do you think Arthur?'

But their friend was staring at the rock face on the other side of the quarry. High above them, about thirty metres up on an impossibly small ledge, stood the Crow Man with his dark-feathered companion perched at his side.

'No way,' Arthur said. 'How did he get there?'

The other two followed his gaze.

For a moment it was like that morning at the Yard. They were mesmerised, held by those eyes even at that distance – and the complete absence of emotion. Even though their opponent was so high up, it felt as if he could launch himself off the ledge.

Time stretched out and the silence expanded until it was broken by a screech from the bird as it swooped down from the quarry wall, wheeling away before turning back towards them. Then a cloud of bats appeared, silently flitting out of the already darkening sky.

It was this that finally snapped Tamar out of her trance. 'Run!' she shouted, as the bats darted and dipped above their heads.

Clutching Mug Shot's lead she sprinted towards the quarry entrance but when she glanced back over her shoulder she realised that Arthur hadn't moved.

'Arthur, come on!'

'Keep going Tamar,' Nick yelled. 'I'll get him.'

Rushing back to Arthur he grasped his sleeve, 'Come on mate.'

Arthur staggered and slipped over the mossy rocks and boulders, forced on by his friend. Above, and to the side of them, a dark shape traversed the quarry face as the previously cloudless sky turned from clear blue to ominous black. A crackle of blinding lightning cut across the sky, swiftly followed by ground-shaking thunder. Rain started to fall. At first it was only a few drops, but within seconds solid sheets of water were emptying out of the sky. They ran, their legs leaden, freezing rain blinding them and driving into their faces.

'Can't see,' Tamar gasped.

'Keep running, don't stop,' Nick yelled, propelling Arthur forward.

He risked a quick look round. They were out of the quarry but now something was on the hillside below them. It was impossible to tell what it was through the downpour. At that moment Arthur skidded on the treacherous ground and glimpsed a low, dark shape out of the corner of his eye and heard a snarl. The rain turned to hail as the wind increased and the snarl became a growl. Arthur's legs and brain felt disconnected; no commands were getting through. He was living through his nightmare.

There was a shout from Nick and he heaved Arthur towards a light on the other side of the track. 'Over there, look!'

As they came closer to the light the shape of a farm cottage, lights winking through the storm, became clearer.

They hammered on the thick, oak door and Mug Shot whimpered, trembling. From inside the cottage came the sounds of movement. There was shuffling and then the sound of a latch being lifted until at last, the door creaked open. A shaft of mellow light and warm air greeted them.

'Well, hello again,' the occupant said, smiling.

Chapter 9

The gift

It was the woman from the bus.

She opened the door wide while looking past them, out into the rain and hail. Her smile was replaced by a frown, as if she had glimpsed something that irritated her.

'You're soaked through,' she said, motioning them inside.

With the door closed the sounds of the storm dulled, and they found themselves in a world more different than they could have imagined. There was something unusual about the cottage. As soon as they'd stepped over the threshold they'd felt it. And somewhere, on the extreme limit of their hearing, there was singing.

'Come right in, don't stand there shiverin',' she said, ushering them towards the fire.

'Don't usually need this in August,' she continued, 't'is unseasonable weather out there.'

'Thanks,' Nick said. 'Yeah, it's pretty bad.'

'It wasn't just the weather,' Tamar remarked, a shake in her voice, 'it was ...'

She hesitated. Somehow describing their experience would make it all the worse, like trying to put a nightmare into words. But their host seemed to understand and, shaking her head, said, 'It's all right m'dears. There's no need to explain.'

She sighed and muttered to herself, 'That woman's at the bottom of this, I'll be bound.'

There was a rattle against the window and a dark shadow passed in front of it.

'Now,' she said briskly, 'you stay there m'dears.'

Hurrying over to the front door she thrust the bolt home into the ancient oak of the doorframe, checked the catch on the window and pulled the curtains closed. No one unwelcome would get into her house. Finally, satisfied with her precautions, their host turned and surveyed them. She stood quietly for a few seconds, with her arms folded and her head inclined, before murmuring something about cake and disappearing into the adjoining room.

***

Everything about the cottage was comfortable, from the wood beams stretching across the low ceiling, to the large, ginger-and-white cat lying in front of the crackling log fire ... the same cat that had been the leader in the Yard. And in a corner of his mind Arthur knew that it was also the cat that had been sitting on his wall. It opened its eyes, calmly assessing them, before lazily yawning and curling into a tight ball.

Meanwhile Mug Shot was in a quandary – he had a difficult choice to make: he could either choose the safety of staying well out of the way of the cat, or sidle closer and enjoy the fire. Eventually the pull of the fire was too much and Tamar watched as he edged forward, turned round once, lay down and started snoring. The cat opened one eye and purred as it saw him settle down.

Tamar nudged Nick. 'I've never seen him do that before!'

'Nope, but that's not a normal cat is it?'

The cat's purr became louder and he fixed them with his green eyes, as if he understood every word they'd said – and agreed.

But Nick's attention was diverted from the cat to a collection of enormous coats and hats hanging by the front door, and several pairs of huge boots beneath them.

He tapped Tamar on the arm and nodded towards the clothes. 'Maybe she lives here with a giant too.'

'She might come back in!' Tamar hissed.

'What? I didn't do anything,' he answered innocently.

Tamar wondered if anything could worry him. They'd been through a terrifying experience and he was still joking.

A grandfather clock ticked in the corner of the room, the chestnut-brown wood gleaming while its pendulum marked time. The face was richly decorated in gold with delicate engravings, and in each corner a painted angel stood out from the clock face.

Throughout Nick and Tamar's conversation Arthur had been examining it. He did a double-take: he was certain one of the angels had moved. Yet even as he looked at the clock his mind was on repeat, endlessly replaying the chase over and over in his head. However much he tried to concentrate on the clock, the images kept flashing up, one after another. The bird swooping, the bats flitting towards them – and the Crow Man perched high on that ledge.

Meanwhile Nick had finished his inspection of the room and was turning his attention to Arthur; his friend hadn't moved an inch. He was just staring at the clock.

'So what do you think he was doing out there?' Tamar asked Nick, while attempting to wring the rain out of her dripping hair.

'Your guess is as good as mine, but I'd lay bets that he wasn't trying to be friendly, or collect stones,' Nick replied briefly, before leaning across to Arthur.

'You okay mate?' He waved his hand in front of Arthur's face.

Tamar and Nick looked at each other. She stopped fiddling with her hair and walked over to Arthur, and crouched down in front of him.

'Arthur?'

But there was no response, so she added casually, 'Hello, anyone in there?'

Their attempts to drag their friend out of his reverie were interrupted by the bustling presence of their now-smiling host entering and carrying a tray stacked with toast, hot chocolate and cake.

'Now m'dears, I'm thinking you could all be doin' with some of this. Draw up closer to the fire.'

She fussed over them, taking their soaked belongings and arranging them so that they could start to dry out.

'Thanks Mrs ...' Nick started.

'Angela Jolly, dear, and it's Miss. I live 'ere with me brother. And you are ... Nick, Tamar and Arthur – and this 'ere is Mug Shot.'

Their surprise at her knowing their names must have shown. Miss Jolly smiled at them. 'We were on the same bus.'

'Oh yes, of course! I thought I recognised you,' Tamar replied.

Angela Jolly had noticed Nick and Tamar's obvious concern for Arthur but, instead of making a fuss, she shook her head and motioned towards the tray.

'I always find good food is worth a thousand words,' she said conversationally.

She gave a large slice of cake to Arthur and offered loaded plates to Nick and Tamar. Then settling herself into a comfortable armchair, she started to make small talk, carefully avoiding any discussion of what had happened on the moor.

'You finished school for the summer, I reckon.'

'D'you all live 'ere abouts?'

Little by little her approach worked. After a while, and much to Tamar and Nick's relief, Arthur started to eat.

'Great cake,' mumbled Nick, his mouth full and scattering crumbs.

'Yeah, lovely!' Tamar agreed. Then she asked, 'Have you always lived up here?'

Angela Jolly replied with a little smile, 'Well, in a way I have. On and off. Some might say forever.'

But any further conversation was brought to an abrupt halt by a thundering on the door. They froze.

Miss Jolly prised herself out of the chair and heaved the iron bolt back. The door creaked open to reveal a man as tall as Angela was short. He was huge. For a few moments all that could be heard was the rhythmic ticking of the clock. The man stood in the doorway with the rain lashing down behind him, surveying the scene in his cottage.

He had the bluest eyes any of them had ever seen, overshadowed by impressive eyebrows in a well-weathered face. All of this was topped by a mane of white hair reaching down to his shoulders.

'Ah, visitors!' he boomed, and strode in, ducking his head to avoid the door lintel. He leant his crook against the wall and called to his dog, 'In, Fly.' Fly bounded in and calmly joined Mug Shot and the cat by the fire.

Angela said, 'Well Michael, you know how to make an entrance an' no mistake!'

'That's as maybe, but are you goin' to interdoos me to our young guests?' he asked, turning towards them after shaking off his vast coat.

Angela introduced him to Nick and Tamar and then Michael turned his attention to Arthur. There was an intensity to the look and, although a smile was lingering, there was no mistaking the concern in his eyes.

Arthur stood up. 'Hi, I'm Arthur,' and his hand was shaken in a bone-crunching grip.

'Ah, Arthur,' was all Michael said in reply. He glanced across the room to his sister.

'So you all came in out of the weather, I take it.'

'Well, yes,' said Nick, helping himself to more cake. 'But there was this odd guy too. We've seen him around town ...'

'Yeah and he was chasing us.' Tamar caught Nick's cautioning look. 'Well he was – and it was really scary.'

'Anyhow, we saw a light and came here,' Nick finished for her.

'I'm pleased you found us,' Miss Jolly said, cutting the cake and handing it to her brother.

'So, he's back,' Michael stated looking at his sister, obviously not doubting their account.

Angela nodded. 'An' if he's back, *she'll* be here too. You mark my words.'

Michael sighed and shook his head. 'Doesn't bode well.'

He turned to them, 'You did well to get 'ere.'

They had mixed feelings. In a way it was affirming to know that their suspicions about the Crow Man were right, but it also brought home that their risk had been a real one – and that they'd had a narrow escape.

Then Miss Jolly exclaimed, 'M'dears, how could I forget? Your folks, they'll be wonderin' where you be.'

They looked at one another. With all that had happened they'd completely forgotten to phone anyone.

Tamar looked at her watch and groaned, 'I'm going to be grounded.' Suddenly that threat seemed more real than the Crow Man.

'I'll phone them,' Nick said, taking charge. Having glanced at Arthur he'd reached the conclusion that his friend was in no state to phone anyone.

As usual he turned on the charm and calmed the situation; most adults fell for it every time. 'No, honestly Mrs Penhaligon, we're all fine … would you? Oh thanks, that'd be great. See you soon, then.'

'Your mum's coming right out, Arthur, and letting everyone know we're not stranded in the middle of the moors. She reckons she'll be about fifteen minutes.'

'Thanks mate!'

'Yeah,' Tamar agreed, 'I didn't fancy being grounded.'

As conversation resumed Michael picked something off a shelf and crossed the room, crouching down beside Arthur.

'Now Arthur,' he said, keeping his voice low against the quiet buzz of easy chatter. 'T'is more than likely that you'll be needin' this.'

Arthur looked at it, frowning.

Michael pressed it into his hand. 'It may come in useful sometime soon.'

'What is it?'

'Look at it,' Michael said, as if it was obvious.

Now turning it over in his hand, Arthur saw that it was an intricately carved whistle.

'Wow, it's great but…' he started, looking puzzled.

'If ever you're up this way, and in difficulty, you must use it.'

Arthur was still doubtful. He couldn't understand how blowing a whistle could get him out of trouble. Even one like this.

Michael chuckled at his expression. 'The dog'll hear it. Fast as the four winds that one be.'

Arthur glanced over to the hearth where Mug Shot was lying, now curled up between Fly and the cat. The animals in this house were unusually accommodating.

Mr Jolly paused briefly before fixing Arthur with a piercing look. 'Be sure to wear it at all times. You never know when you'll need it – or how your call will be answered.'

Arthur tucked the whistle under his T-shirt and frowned, 'Will we see you again then?'

Michael paused as if he was considering what he should say. Eventually he replied, 'I can't say what the future will bring lad, but I've a feelin' you will … and I've a feelin' it won't be a long wait.'

Their conversation was interrupted by a hesitant knocking.

'That'll be your mother, Arthur,' Miss Jolly said, heaving herself out of her armchair.

'That was quick!' Tamar exclaimed. 'I'm sure we only phoned a couple of minutes ago.

'The hour sometimes has its own time in this 'ouse,' Angela replied, as she unlocked the door.

Nick and Tamar looked at each other wondering what she meant, but before they could ask they found themselves being ushered towards the door. So, again, it was only Arthur who caught a glimpse of the angels in the clock nodding in agreement as he stood up to follow the others to the car. He decided that they must be mechanical or something; there was no way that they could possibly move by themselves.

However, he might have been convinced if he'd seen the minute hand of the grandfather clock start to pick up speed until it was a blur, before slowing down to resume its usual pace.

Time, it appeared, did not have to be subject to the usual laws in this house.

Chapter 10

Ghost image

As they sped home, Arthur sat in the back of the car with his face pressed to the window, mulling over all that had happened. He looked up at the black clouds being blown away to reveal a rose-tinted sky. There was little trace now of the summer storm. Snippets of conversation flowed over him, scarcely penetrating his thoughts.

'What lovely people!' Mrs Penhaligon was remarking. 'Fancy letting you lot in.'

'Yeah, they're brother and sister,' Tamar informed her. 'And Angela makes the most amazing cakes.'

'I guessed that; Nick's got quite a bit on his sweatshirt,' she said smiling. 'By the way, what happened to your phones? Couldn't you get a signal?'

'Um, well, –' Arthur started.

'When the rain started, we just ran for it,' Tamar cut in.

'Yeah,' Nick continued, thinking fast. 'And their house was near. We weren't thinking straight. Once we were in there we almost forgot about the weather.'

Mrs Penhaligon glanced in the rear-view mirror at Arthur. 'What was that you said about phoning if you needed anyone? Knocking on a strangers' door isn't the wisest move – unless it's an emergency … even if they do turn out to be kind and give you cake.'

'Sorry,' Arthur mumbled.

The three youngsters stared ahead, not wanting to admit that it *had* been an emergency. They had an unspoken agreement that the Crow Man and the chase were not going to be mentioned. At least not for now.

However, as the car wound back down the lanes towards their homes the day's events continued to run through Arthur's mind, fragmented like stills from a video. He kept seeing that bird launching itself off the cliff and his own paralysis and sense of powerlessness, but as these thoughts threatened to overwhelm him he was once again in the safety of the cottage. He held the thread around his neck. It was a reminder of a real promise of help – if ever he should need it. He hoped he wouldn't.

But the conversation had moved on; Mrs Penhaligon was talking, 'The Police called. There's no sign of that man. They reckon he was a tramp and is probably miles away by now.'

They looked at one another and Nick raised an eyebrow but said nothing. The car rumbled over a cattle grid.

'Oh, and by the way Tamar, your mum's in a bit of a state,' Mrs Penhaligon said.

'Why? Because we were caught in the storm?'

'No. Well, that bothered her of course. But an odd thing happened this afternoon …'

'What? I mean in what way?' Tamar asked, pulling Mug Shot closer.

'Well, I don't think it's that odd, so don't worry, but it unsettled your mum. A bird flew into the kitchen window.

She was at the sink so you would have thought it could have seen her.'

'Probably a short-sighted bird,' Nick said, grinning at Arthur. But his smile disappeared when he saw Arthur's expression.

'Anyway,' Mrs Penhaligon continued as she steered the car into Nick's road. 'I gather it left an imprint on the window almost like a ghost image. They do sometimes you know. It was huge apparently. Lucky it didn't break the window.'

She stopped the car. 'It just left a mound of black feathers, I'm amazed it was even able to fly off!'

'What sort of bird was it?' Nick asked, as he opened the car door.

'Oh, a crow I should imagine,' Mrs Penhaligon replied, dismissing further discussion. 'Bye dear. It's your day with your dad tomorrow, isn't it?'

Nick nodded, lost for words.

'Have a good time. I'm sure you will,' she added comfortingly.

As she pulled away Arthur turned round. Nick hadn't moved, he was just standing looking after them.

The remainder of the drive was completed in silence. Mrs Penhaligon was completely oblivious to the emotions her words had stirred up. Pulling up in front of Tamar's house she said, 'I should go and make your mum a nice cup of tea dear, that'll calm her nerves.'

Arthur thought wryly what high hopes his mum placed in the restorative qualities of a tea-bag. If only she knew!

Tamar smiled weakly. 'I might try that Mrs Penhaligon. Thanks for the lift.'

She stepped out of the car, pulling Mug Shot after her, while Mrs Penhaligon lavished the usual affection on the dog. When Tamar turned to wave, Arthur was struck with how pale she looked.

***

Arthur closed his front door and glanced around the hallway as if he was seeing it for the first time.

He took in the photos hanging on the walls, cataloguing family holidays, and the piles of boots and shoes by the door. It all felt so normal. The low murmur of the television drifted from the front room, so Arthur wandered in. His dad was sprawled on the settee with his mouth wide open, fast asleep and snoring.

'*Nothing unusual there then,*' he thought, thankful that the usual pattern of things remained unchanged here – if nowhere else.

He slumped into a chair. The local news was on and an enthusiastic, fresh-faced reporter was smiling into the camera.

'Today has been an extraordinary day up here on Bodmin Moor,' she was saying. Arthur sat up and leant forward, frowning.

The camera panned back to take in the countryside behind her. There was a glimpse of mine buildings and some ancient standing stones. Then it returned to the reporter, now with three local people at her side.

She made a brief introduction, describing a 'freak' storm, the most unusual in living memory. Apparently it was likely to 'Break all records!'

She turned to the first interviewee and, thrusting the microphone in front of him, asked, 'Well, Mr Harris, you're a local farmer up here on the moors. I imagine farming must be hard under the best conditions but today must have been a nightmare!'

'Too right!' Arthur mumbled.

The bearded farmer, in his tweed jacket and flat cap, nodded. He'd obviously had a memorable day as well.

'I've never seen anything like it in all my days! 'Ere we be in August and we be 'aving hail the size of cricket balls!'

He added that 'bucket loads' of the stuff had rained down on him during the storm, even injuring some of his sheep! He shook his head before adding, 'T'aint normal, make no mistake t'is the start of somethin' momentous!'

A second person, an expert on the history of the moors, half-moon glasses precariously balanced on his nose, described how an old tree generally agreed to be almost five hundred years old, had been split in two by lightning, 'As if by a mighty axe!'

This tree was up in the region of the standing stones called, 'Arthur's Hall'. It was supposed to be linked to the ancient and mythical King of Cornwall, and this, according to the historian, made it even more portentous.

With a cheery smile and a 'Thank you for that Mr Pendower,' the reporter turned to her last interviewee.

'Mrs Trebartha has also had a most unusual experience – they say these things come in threes! Would you like to describe to the viewers exactly what you saw today?'

Indeed, Mrs Trebartha was very keen to tell everyone about her sighting of the Beast of Bodmin Moor.

'It was as clear as day! Frightened me 'alf to death, I'll be tellin' you. Well, least thing you'd be expectin' when you be out for a quiet walk.' Folding her arms to rest on an immense bosom she grumbled, 'My poor little dog is still in shock. Look at 'er!'

The camera moved to take in the quivering animal. Although to Arthur's eyes it was more rat than dog.

'I'm sure it must have been startling!' agreed the reporter.

'Well, I think this day will be remembered for many years,' she said, turning to the camera. 'This is Susie Mawgan for Kernow Television, on the wilds of Bodmin Moor.'

Arthur thought that if she was announcing World War III she'd probably remark on what an interesting day it had been for all concerned.

He glowered at the television. 'Too right it'll be remembered!' he said, jabbing at the remote control as he switched off the TV.

It was becoming clear to him that events were heating up. He'd become more and more certain that in some way he was inextricably involved. He was the one the Crow Man had appeared to most of all; he'd even been in his house! And Michael had singled him out to give him that whistle. It was as if he knew that something dangerous was going to happen. Arthur had a creeping realisation that he was going to have to do something more. He had no idea what it was, but he still felt it was something to do with the quarry. And this time he wasn't going to drag his friends into it.

He was going to go it alone.

Chapter 11

The first endeavour

However, Arthur's plans had to change because Nick's dad couldn't make his prearranged visit the next day.

'Work or something – as usual,' Nick said dismissively, at the other end of the phone.

He didn't talk about it much, but Arthur knew how Nick felt whenever these arrangements fell through. Immediately he decided that his own plans could wait. It was sunny so the only option was the beach; neither the Yard nor the moors were possible now.

'How about going down to the coast?' he suggested. 'We could go to Pendrym.'

'Cool – we haven't done that for ages,' Nick said. Usually it was his last choice but today it seemed perfect. His dad always sent round some money as a sort of peace offering when his plans altered; he'd use that.

'Tell you what, you text Tamar and see if she's up for it,' Arthur said. 'I don't think she'd be too keen if she knew it was another of my ideas.'

'You know,' Nick replied, 'I think you *might* be right. Okay, I'll meet you at the station in an hour. There's a train around then.'

Arthur put Michael's gift around his neck and tucked it under his T-shirt. Although he still couldn't see how it would help in a crisis, it was strangely comforting to have it with him.

As he left the house he glanced up at the window of the house opposite. He'd found himself doing that more and more recently, as if there was some connection between its owner and all that was happening. But there was no movement that he could see. He set off down his street on the look-out for anything unusual, but everything seemed normal; no cats lined the road anyway.

Behind him a woman came to the window of the house opposite his and watched him walk down the road. Then she sat at her desk, dipped a feathered pen in green ink and began Writing.

***

At the arranged time the three friends were on Lyskeret station platform. Tamar had left Mug Shot behind because he had a fascination for seagulls and she'd decided that she could do without a hyperactive dog today.

'So how was your mum?' Arthur asked Tamar as they sat on the bench in the quiet country station.

'Well, she'd calmed down by the time I got back. But look at this feather; I would definitely say it's from a crow.'

She took a jet-black feather out of her bag and handed it to the boys.

They looked at it carefully. However, they both knew that it needed no further identification.

'So where does that leave us?' Nick asked, looking at Arthur.

'Not sure,' Arthur replied. He was determined that the next stage of this mystery was going to be up to him. There was no way he would draw his friends into it again.

'A murder of crows,' he muttered to himself.

'What?' Tamar asked.

'Oh, that's what they call a group of crows,' Arthur said, turning the feather over in his hands. 'Most other birds are called flocks; not crows, though.'

'Great, you've made the day feel that little bit better!' she retorted, a little shaken.

'Sorry,' he said. 'Just thinking, that's all.'

'Thinking is seriously overrated,' Nick remarked.

At that point the little two-carriage train drew into sight cutting short any further discussion. They climbed on and sat among holiday-makers unused to being able to take a short train ride to the sea, and excited chattering surrounded them.

As the train travelled through the valley and alongside the tidal river to the coast, Arthur leant against the window, rocking with the motion of the carriage.

Lost in his thoughts he idly traced the carvings on the whistle beneath his shirt, slowly becoming aware that his chest was feeling cool where the whistle lay. Then up above the train he noticed a dark bird keeping pace with the engine. His heart sank. Surely nothing more could happen today. At that moment the train burst out of the wooded valley into the small seaside town and the bird disappeared.

'Come on,' Tamar said to him, 'we're here.'

Arthur decided not to mention the bird, and he preferred not to think about the whistle cooling. That was way too weird.

The train slowed to a stop and the passengers poured on to the station platform. The friends gathered their bags and, with the other day-trippers, made their way through Pendrym town and its bustling harbour. They ambled past the fishing boats with their boxes of glassy-eyed, wide-mouthed fish on the decks and other boats with their nets spread out. Overhead, seagulls screeched and wheeled in the salty breeze.

'Let's go to the beach. I can't be bothered with the shops yet,' Tamar said. 'But I need to drop in to that little gift shop later. I'd like to get something for Mum after yesterday.'

So they followed the masses down to the town's beach with its trampolines and rides, and its soft sand and deep blue sea.

'Lovely day,' Nick observed. He didn't add that his dad was missing out on the sun, although he thought it.

'Yeah, it's perfect,' Tamar agreed.

They arranged their towels and sat and chatted and soaked up the sun.

Tamar mentioned a book she was reading, which reminded Arthur of the leather-bound book in Nick's house. 'By the way Nick,' he said, 'I'd almost forgotten – who gave you that book?'

'Which book?'

'That leather one that was on your kitchen windowsill.'

'Oh, that one! It was the new history teacher. You know the tall one with the little round glasses,' Nick replied.

Arthur was intrigued. 'Why did she give it to you?'

'Search me,' Nick shrugged. 'She said something about it being useful to me, or us. I can't remember!'

'Have you looked at it?' Tamar asked.

'No! I'm not into books.'

Tamar turned to Arthur. 'Hasn't she moved in opposite you? I'm sure I saw her there the other day.'

'Yeah, she might have.' It hadn't even occurred to him

that the new neighbour was their teacher. As Tamar frequently complained, he was a bit of a bloke when it came to recognising faces. Although, he recalled, he hadn't actually seen the face of the neighbour.

'She's cool though isn't she?' Tamar said.

'Only if you like history!' Nick grumbled.

'She's keen on ancient Greece and Egypt, and she was teaching us about some of our local history the other day in history club. Honestly, she made it come alive … it was almost as if she'd been there!' Tamar enthused.

Nick cast a doubtful look in her direction. He couldn't understand how anyone could enjoy history, let alone voluntarily attend an after-school club about it. But Arthur thought about the teacher and how she'd repeatedly appeared in his classes. Usually she was giving a message, or delivering a note or a book to someone in his class; but every time he'd looked at her, she seemed to be focused on something else. He decided that the next time he was at Nick's house he'd have a proper look at that book.

He lay back and thought about all the weird things that were happening around him. But soon he was drifting, the events of the past few days receding and everyday sounds fading to be replaced by disjointed words.

***

The Writer sat on a bench on the small promenade at the top of the beach. Her hands were folded in her lap, her glasses hung around her neck and her grey hair was pulled back and tied neatly on the top of her head. No one gave her a second glance, which was exactly what she wanted. She watched Arthur and his friends as they chatted at the far end of the beach, and she listened to their conversation. There were times when the ability to hear words spoken from far off could be distracting – when all she desired was silence. But she had work to do and she needed to hear those words.

She smiled quietly to herself when she heard Tamar's enthusiasm for her subject. Perhaps one day Tamar would see some of these sights for herself – then history really *would* come alive.

The Writer knew that the path that lay ahead for the three friends was not an easy one. She considered others whose paths she'd documented over the years and was immediately transported back to the time when she'd listened to the words of that strangely wonderful man, Albert Einstein. Now, he'd been an interesting subject; his words had never been dull! Her thoughts wandered as she recollected his sayings; he'd had such an original, creative mind.

The Writer leant back, allowing herself a moment's reminiscence and enjoying the sun and the seemingly innocent scene in front of her, when a shadow flitted overhead. She looked up. The bird was back. She sighed, reached into a large bag at her side and pulled out a heavy, leather-bound book.

***

Suddenly Arthur was wide awake – something was different. He looked around, up and down the beach. There were children making sand-castles and people paddling and swimming. Everything looked completely normal, but he was beginning to recognise this feeling too well. He leant over to his backpack and slipped his hand into the pocket where he'd put the whistle for safety. Even though the sun was shining, the whistle was bitterly cold. He put it around his neck ... just in case. He glanced around again; this time he noticed a dark shape soaring high overhead and the usual clamour of seagulls had disappeared. It was time to move. He felt like a sitting target and he wasn't in the mood to be one again.

'You've woken up!' Tamar said. 'Shame, Nick was going to help you.'

'Cheers guys,' Arthur replied. Then he added casually, 'Actually ... I think we probably ought to be going.'

'What! Already?' Nick exclaimed.

'Yes, already,' Arthur retorted – a little more abruptly than he'd intended.

Nick was about to say something but Tamar put her hand on his arm. She'd seen the look on Arthur's face.

'Okay,' she said nonchalantly, 'I need to pop into that shop anyway.'

She stood up and, turning her back to Arthur, cast a look at Nick. Tamar could see that he was still about to come out with some comment. She frowned and shook her head at him while she shoved her towel into her backpack.

Nick glanced at Arthur. His friend was pale. Something had spooked him. So for once, Nick bit back any of his usual remarks, and the three of them made their way up the crowded beach to the pavement. They sauntered inland, back along the road that followed the line of the tidal river feeding into the sea.

Arthur looked at the sky. Dark clouds were gathering and the light breeze was whipping up into an angry wind. People had been sitting along the harbour-side, dangling baited lines into the fast-moving river with buckets of scuttling crabs by their sides. But now the river was being stirred up, the holiday-makers were moving away.

'You've done well there, kid,' Nick remarked to one boy with a seething bucket of crabs. 'How d'you manage to catch all of them?'

The freckle-faced boy was about to launch into an earnest explanation when a scream pierced the air.

'Kensa!'

They stopped dead in their tracks.

A young mother was standing petrified at the harbour's edge. Her little girl had fallen into the turbulent river which, now the tide had turned, was a boiling mass of water.

'I can't swim!' her mother was shouting while people around her looked on, horrified. 'Someone – help me! Please!'

'She won't stand a chance,' Tamar said, appalled. 'Where's the lifebelt?'

'There's no time for that,' replied Nick. 'Look at the speed of the water.'

'Well someone's got to do something!'

But in that instant Arthur understood that this was a personal challenge. He was the one who had to save her.

It took only a moment's hesitation for him to thrust his bag at Nick, kick his shoes off and sprint to the edge of the churning water and then dive in.

The river had claimed its prize.

Chapter 12

A pale stranger

Arthur hit the icy water and gasped with the shock of it … and sank like a stone. Paralysed by the freezing river, he was pulled under by the strength of the turning tide. Seaweed brushed his face and hands, fish darted past him, and then, once again, he was high in the sky – looking down at his body floating above the river-bed. He was wondering how this could be possible, and was quite ready to drift away, when something nudged him and he was pulled back to his body only to find himself gazing into the enormous eyes of an Atlantic grey seal.

His lungs felt as though they were about to explode but the seal was positioning itself, tucking its muzzle under his arm (Arthur could even feel its whiskers), and he was being guided upwards, propelled towards the light.

Arthur hit the surface gasping for air. Miraculously he'd resurfaced within arm's reach of the tiny girl, but a couple more seconds and she'd be beyond his grasp. He hadn't time to recoup his strength, he had to move now.

'Here!' he shouted, and struck out towards her.

But it was as if the river, sensing it would lose the child to Arthur, re-doubled its efforts. A vicious current seized Kensa, sweeping her from his outstretched hands.

Despair washed over him. It was taking all his strength to stay afloat never mind rescue the little girl. He was so stupid to have even tried. What had possessed him! There was no way that he could catch her; he was no match for these conditions. But then a pair of piercing blue eyes flashed in front of him and, deep in his brain, he was certain that he heard a conversation.

'He's The One,' a voice was saying.

'Yes, he's been Chosen,' said another.

And Arthur knew – he didn't know how he knew; he just did – that the voices were talking about him, and that he had to try to save the little girl whatever may happen. So calling on every last reserve of energy, he struck out against the power of the river and made a desperate lunge in Kensa's direction. Unbelievably his fingers caught the very edge of her T-shirt.

'He's got her!' he heard someone shout and a cry went up from the crowd at the harbour's edge.

'Don't worry, we'll make it,' he panted, hauling her towards him.

The little girl, shocked and cold, didn't say anything but just lay limply in his arms. By now he was so exhausted that he was barely treading water. Then once again he felt the seal beside him. In one fluid move it buoyed him up and pushed them towards the harbour wall.

Arthur heard exclamations and cries from the crowd and with renewed strength he turned on to his back. He kicked out while firmly holding the shivering child and swam and fought against the powerful current. Thinking about it later, he wondered if it had been more than just the river working against him. It felt as though hands were grasping his feet and reaching for his ankles.

'I'm going to do this,' he said grimly to himself. 'No one, nothing, is going to stop me now.'

From the quayside there were shouts of encouragement. Then, and just for a moment, he thought he caught a glimpse of someone who looked remarkably like Michael Jolly.

'Right kid, we're nearly there!' Arthur said, more for his own benefit than Kensa's.

And yet again the seal appeared at his side and, slipping under his arm, steered him towards safety.

***

A loud cheer echoed along the quay and helping hands reached out and lifted them to safety. Two police officers had arrived and Kensa's mum was in the middle of the crowd with her arms outstretched, calling out to her tiny daughter as she was passed towards her.

As Arthur was being hauled out of the water he glanced over his shoulder and caught a glimpse of the seal disappearing under the water ... and raising a flipper. *Now I really am losing it,* he thought, as he was hoisted out of the river by a policeman into the waiting crowd.

'Well done, boy!' A strapping fisherman slapped him on the back. 'You did it! Proper job.'

Other people were crowding around wanting to congratulate him, but Kensa's mother appeared and the policeman stood back and the crowd parted to let her through. She was clutching her shivering daughter, already wrapped in a towel, to her chest.

Before he had time to stop her, she'd enveloped Arthur in a massive hug, 'Thank you so very, very much!'

'Hey, no problem,' Arthur mumbled through his shivers.

'I don't know what happened,' she continued, wiping away tears. 'One minute I was holding her hand and the next she was in the water.'

'Oh, kids can be quick,' Arthur replied mechanically. He was completely drained and beyond any meaningful conversation.

'No,' she persisted, 'it was more than that.' She paused and took a breath. 'It was as if someone had deliberately taken her hand.'

Arthur looked up sharply. 'What d'you mean?'

'I was holding her hand really firmly because I know this river, but then it felt ... it felt like her hand was taken out of my hand.'

The tiny girl whimpered and knotted her arms around her mother's neck and a sigh escaped from the crowd. Arthur thought for a few seconds. He was certain that there was more to this than met the eye. And then his attention was drawn to the back of the throng that had gathered, and to a man who, even in a busy crowd, stood out from all those surrounding him.

The girl's mother was still talking. 'I feel so guilty.'

'Look, I know ... in fact I'm sure, it wasn't your fault,' Arthur replied, scrutinising the stranger.

There was something different about this man. It wasn't only his appearance which was unusual – his long fair hair and dark eyes – but his stance. He was leaning against the wall with his arms folded and seemed completely relaxed; however, he was examining Arthur with an intensity which reminded him of the Crow Man.

Arthur shifted his attention back to the young woman. 'Listen!' he stated emphatically. 'You've got to believe me when I say it wasn't your fault. There are some vicious people around, but Kensa's safe now and I think you need to get back to the rest of your family. Look they're all waiting for you!'

Kensa's mother glanced away just as the policeman came up to her saying that he needed to take some details and it would be advisable to get Kensa to a doctor. And immediately Arthur took his chance and slipped into the crowd, avoiding the policewoman who was making a beeline for him. He wasn't being rude, he would have liked to say a proper 'goodbye' to Kensa and her mum, but he was desperate to escape the scrutiny of the stranger. He looked over his shoulder, wondering about the identity of the fair-haired man, but he'd gone.

***

Viatoris Watched.

He'd taken in the angry river and the pale one, Hagarawall. He smiled with a grim satisfaction. Seal had done well.

It was hard having to Watch when the odds were so high, but the Rule was that no interference was allowed. He was a Watcher and, if help came, it wasn't permitted to come from him. He had to let events take their course. His role was to take note of all that happened; of all that was destined. But he was certain now – this boy was The One.

***

Thoughts and ideas jostled against one another, vying for Arthur's attention but there were too many to make any kind of sense.

'That was amazing!' Nick exclaimed. 'I didn't know you could swim like that. How did you do it?'

But Arthur was too tired for further conversation so he just shrugged and dragged a dry T-shirt out of his backpack. Wearily he pushed his feet into his trainers and checked that the whistle was still around his neck.

Tamar agreed, 'Yes, that was brilliant Arthur!'

She wanted to give him a hug but she held back. She didn't want to give Nick any reason to tease her, instead she just said, 'Come on guys, how about a hot chocolate? Oh and I fancy some chips, or cake, or toast, or maybe ...' She stopped mid-sentence. 'What?'

Nick was staring open-mouthed. 'I thought I was the only one who was that interested in food!'

'Not just for me, idiot, for Arthur. Look, he's about to pass out!'

Nick looked at Arthur. He was shivering and blue with cold. 'Ah yeah, but mate, was that a seal out there?'

'Nick!'

'Okay, okay,' he held up his hands in mock surrender. 'Let's go then.'

Arthur took his backpack from Nick and started walking away from the treacherous river just as the policewoman caught up with him. He sighed. He tried to be polite but there was no way he was going to have a check-up at the hospital, as she was suggesting, or be driven home, when all he needed was a hot drink. (And time to think.)

Eventually he said, 'Okay ... look, I'll take your card, and I give you my word that I'll phone you if I need help.'

She still looked concerned and said sternly, 'Well, please make sure you do.' And reluctantly, realising that she wasn't going to win this battle, she turned to Tamar and Nick, 'Will you keep an eye on him for me, please? Shock can be very dangerous. Too many people underestimate it.'

They nodded and promised to call her if he felt ill – and Arthur breathed out; they were free to go! But the crowd still lingered and, winding their way through, Arthur's hair was ruffled and his back slapped more times than he could count, but he was only faintly aware of all of this. His thoughts were focused on what lengths somebody, or something, would go to in an attempt to endanger him.

Or anybody else unfortunate enough to be nearby.

Chapter 13

Guided

Trudging through the winding lanes packed with holiday-makers, Nick kept casting curious sideways glances at Arthur, waiting for an opportunity to question him some more about what he'd seen. However, Tamar was on a one-woman mission to pump food into their friend and even Nick knew that had to come first.

'Let's go in here,' Tamar said, dragging Arthur by the arm into a warm café. 'I've been here before – they do hot chocolate with more cream than should be legal.'

'Sounds good,' Arthur said, although really he was beyond caring.

'I thought you were eating healthily over the summer,' Nick teased Tamar.

'That's on hold,' she replied curtly, leading them to a quiet corner at the back of the café. 'Come on, I could do with an excuse and I reckon Arthur's earned it for all of us.' She handed a menu to Arthur. 'This one's on us,' she said, and smiled sweetly at Nick.

He grunted his assent; it was the only possible answer.

It didn't take long to make their choices and, ten minutes later as they were eating fries and drinking hot chocolate, Arthur felt some life returning to him, just in time to field a telephone call from his anxious mum saying she'd heard from the policewoman – and should she come and fetch him and take him to a doctor?

He gathered his minimal acting skills. 'No, honestly, I'm fine, Mum. I had some dry clothes with me.'

He listened for a bit before adding, 'Yes I know, it's important to get warm, that's why we're in a café having hot chocolate.'

There was more chatter from his mum before he rolled his eyes, saying, 'No Mum, I promise, I won't get into any *more* trouble.' He made a desperate face at Tamar who grinned back at him. 'Yes, okay, I'll see you later.'

He sighed, shaking his head, and shoved the phone into the pocket of his backpack as he muttered, 'Why does she think it's all *my* fault?'

Tamar picked at some cake crumbs. 'Well, seeing it from her point of view, the last few days have been pretty dramatic. You can't blame her for being worried.'

Arthur sighed again. 'I know, but it's not as if we chose to be stalked by a weird guy and a bird – or have a kid fall in the river right in front of us!'

Quietly, they contemplated all that had happened until Nick finally broke the silence with the question he'd been so desperate to ask: 'So, was that a seal out there, or was I seeing things?'

'What? Oh no, you're right, it was a seal,' Arthur replied, running his finger around the rim of his mug.

'A seal?' Tamar scooped some of the cream off the top of her hot chocolate. 'But I thought they never came up the river.'

'They don't usually.'

'So what was it doing there then?'

Arthur shrugged. 'Search me.'

But Nick was watching him; he knew more had happened than Arthur was willing to let on. However, their conversation was brought to a halt by a demanding bark. Sitting at the open doorway of the café, a black and white collie dog waited with its eyes trained on Arthur.

Now it had his attention, it barked while looking over its shoulder, back down the lane. Then it stood up and barked again, this time more urgently. Inside his shirt Arthur could feel the whistle against his chest. This time it felt warm.

That's really odd, he thought. *How does it do that?*

Looking at the dog he heard himself saying, 'Think it's time to be going guys, sorry!'

'It's like being with an animal whisperer,' Nick joked, but even he was beginning to understand that something mysterious was going on and that he should trust Arthur's instincts.

They finished their drinks and made their way to the front of the café and the open door where the dog was waiting for them. As they approached, it barked once and set off down the lane.

'I think he wants us to follow him,' Tamar said, and added, 'I never thought people said that in real life.'

'Normal people don't,' Arthur replied with some feeling.

From time to time the dog looked over his shoulder, checking that they were still with him, until he came to a small shop and sat down on the pavement.

'What now?' Nick asked.

'Um, I think we're meant to go in,' Arthur said. 'Isn't this the place you wanted to come to anyway, Tamar?'

'Oh yes, it is! Now that *is* different, a dog that can mind-read!' she said. 'Mug Shot's going to be dead jealous.'

'Don't suppose we'll have to tell it to stay,' Nick mused.

At which point the dog lay down, rested his head on his front legs and fixed them with a pair of brown eyes.

'Nope, rather think it'll tell us what we should be doing!' Tamar remarked, and pushed at the door.

Arthur paused to stroke the dog's head as he followed the others into a dark, low-ceilinged room. A bell rang, announcing their arrival. They looked around. Every available surface was covered with curios and ornaments, and the bay windows were so cluttered that the light had to battle to make its way through the glass. The street sounds faded. If it weren't for some of the displays, they could have been in another century. Arthur had been told that some of the cottages in Pendrym were built from the timbers of ancient sailing ships, so maybe that would explain the sense of timelessness.

Tamar and Nick were quickly distracted by the bright mugs for sale at the front of the shop and started picking them up and discussing them – for once without any arguments. But Arthur wasn't interested in souvenirs for tourists; he'd noticed something far more interesting at the back of the shop.

He nudged past shelves full of faded books, glancing at their titles – many of them were about jousting or ancient myths and legends – and past a locked glass cabinet full of semi-precious stones. Squeezing between a rack of maps and another bookshelf, he arrived at a display of sculpted mythical figures and medieval knights. Some of them were mounted on horseback; others wielded a lance or a sword. Many were painted, but a couple were quite plain and carved from stone and it was these that drew his attention.

Picking one up, he turned it over in his hands, his mind making connections with this model and the gift he'd been given by his Great-Uncle Lance.

'Ah, interested in times past then, sir?'

Arthur spun round. He hadn't seen anyone in the shop, but a short, round man, peering over spectacles lodged on the end of his nose, was standing next to him. Arthur scanned the room and now realised that there was a low doorway at the back of the shop. Framed there was a boy of about his age with long, ungainly limbs and a shock of dark hair.

'Hi,' Arthur said, somewhat unnerved by this silent observer.

But before the boy was allowed to answer, Arthur's attention was dragged back to the shopkeeper as the model was gently taken out of his hands.

'How about this one, sir?' the man suggested, replacing it with another from the shelf.

There was a movement in the doorway and the boy had disappeared.

'Is that your son?'

'Who? Oh, Gawain, no … well not exactly. Now, you'll have to be careful with this one, sir.'

'What?'

He was holding a model, of a knight brandishing a sword, out to Arthur. 'This one's rather special.'

'What? But I don't …' Arthur was confused. He hadn't been about to buy anything and there was something about the boy. It felt as though they'd met somewhere before.

'Er, well,' Arthur started, glancing back to the now empty doorway, 'I wasn't actually …'

'You weren't actually …?'

'Well, I haven't got enough money with me.'

'Ah, I see,' replied the man, smiling. 'But I wasn't expecting you to pay for it! This is a gift. You may find it useful.'

'Useful?'

Perhaps this man was even more eccentric than he'd first appeared. How could a stone model possibly be useful? And why would a shopkeeper just give it to him?

'Of course, but you'll find that out at some point, sir.'

With that he thrust the model at Arthur while nodding towards the door.

'I think it's time for you to be going,' the man remarked, not unkindly.

Arthur could see the dog through the glass, sitting up and ready to move on, but Tamar had found something she wanted. As she approached the shopkeeper the dog whined, stretching.

'Take that for your mother, young lady. No cost.'

'What, are you sure? Hey, how did you know it's for Mum?'

Tamar was looking puzzled but the shopkeeper seemed oblivious to her questions and confusion. Instead he was becoming agitated and obviously had other things on his mind.

'Yes, yes, you must be on your way,' he replied, ushering them towards the door. He surveyed the street muttering, 'Not much time though.'

With that he patted the dog, 'Speed beneath your paws.'

He briefly touched Arthur on the shoulder instructing, 'Hold on to that model, sir.'

'Yes ...' Arthur replied, baffled. 'Okay. Thanks.'

The dog was already down the road and looking over his shoulder he barked, willing them to hurry. A sense of urgency filled them and without any further discussion they found themselves running down the street, keeping pace with their guide. The dog burst out of the old streets and raced towards the station. Once or twice they looked behind, but there was no one who appeared to be a threat.

They shot into the little station just as the train was about to close its doors. The dog bounded into the first carriage he came to, barking and tail wagging, with Nick, Arthur and Tamar just behind him as the station master slammed the door shut. The train juddered and moved away from the platform, but as it rounded a corner of the track Arthur glanced out of the window.

Watching the train were the Crow Man and his black-feathered companion.

They'd only just made it.

Chapter 14

Going solo

It was misty, which was far from ideal for what he had in mind, but as Arthur sat swaying with the motion of the village bus he knew he was doing the right thing. There could be no turning back now.

As the bus pulled itself up the hills, Arthur thought through all that had happened and checked again that the whistle was around his neck and that the model was in his pocket; although he couldn't for the life of him see what possible help that could be.

He looked down at the dog and wondered who he could belong to. By the time they'd got back from their trip it had been too late to do anything about finding his owner, so Arthur's parents had eventually agreed that they could phone around in the morning to try to find out where he lived. And Arthur had another reason to be grateful to the animal, because his presence had neatly succeeded in distracting his mum and dad from his near-drowning.

However, this morning the dog had refused to be left behind, so they'd crept out of the house together. Arthur had left a scribbled note saying he'd taken the dog for a walk, which in a way was true enough – and it would give him time to follow up his idea. The dog looked up at him and barked quietly as if he was reading Arthur's thoughts.

'Yeah, I guess you've got a job to do,' Arthur said. 'One man and his dog, eh? Anyway, what am I going to call you?' He was in no doubt now that the dog was meant to stay with him. His mum had already fallen in love with him, so Arthur could foresee only token resistance from that quarter.

He thought through some names as he ruffled the animal's ears; there was no way that the usual ones would suit him and Rover was definitely out! This dog was too much of a free spirit, and far too intelligent, to be insulted by something so unimaginative.

'I know,' Arthur said, 'how about Lightning?'

The dog wagged his tail approvingly and Arthur thought that it was probably just as well that Nick and Tamar weren't there. He'd never live down asking a dog what it would like to be called. He smiled to himself and turned to look out of the window, only to realise that the mist was getting thicker and the sky was growing even darker. His heart sank.

The bus slowed down and, shuddering, came to a halt.

Arthur was the only passenger and as he climbed down, the driver turned to him and leant on the wheel. 'No friends today?'

'No, they've let me out by myself.'

'Well, you take care now,' the driver continued. 'Been 'avin' some terrible weather up here.'

'Yeah, I know!' Arthur agreed, thinking back to the afternoon that had ended at the Jollys' house.

'Been on telly an' all.' Looking at the sky, the driver added, 'Wouldn't be surprised if we 'ad more of the same today.'

He surveyed the mist in front of him, sniffed, threw the bus into gear and lurched away with a quick wave before swiftly disappearing into the swirling cloud.

***

Arthur listened to the sound of the bus fading into the distance and looked at the mist.

It was so much thicker at this height that shapes were quickly swallowed up in it. One minute you could see something, the next it was gone. He wished he'd remembered his compass because losing your sense of direction was too easy in these conditions, but at least he had his phone. He touched the whistle hung around his neck and remembered Michael Jolly's promise.

Arthur started up the track towards the quarry with his eyes glued to the ground, taking care not to stray off the path. He was making for an ancient house deep in the heart of the moor. He'd remembered it during the night and had a feeling that there was something important about it. Something to do with the name. His teacher had mentioned it on that field trip, but he couldn't remember what it was, so eventually he'd decided that he had to come out and find out for himself.

The track was damp and the stones were slippery. Shapes loomed at him, turning into ponies or sheep as they came nearer, and then silently moved away.

At first Arthur met some other walkers. He was ridiculously pleased to see them but soon realised that they were all walking in the opposite direction to him; hiking down the path, away from the quarry, and back towards civilisation. They looked curiously at the boy out alone in such conditions, but he just smiled at them with a confidence that was far from the way he was feeling.

But one man, wearing a flat cap with silver curls escaping from under the brim, stopped.

'You out 'ere on your own, boy?'

Arthur nodded.

The man looked closely at him.

Arthur noticed that his dark eyes twinkled and he was instantly reminded of Michael and Angela Jolly. Furthermore he was carrying a delicately carved walking stick and the carving bore a striking resemblance to the whistle which Michael had given him. As he registered this, the old man's gaze was drawn to the strand of thread peeping from the neck of Arthur's sweatshirt.

'Ah, you be Arthur then. I thought as much.'

'How do you know my name?' Arthur asked, reaching towards Lightning.

The man chuckled. 'Your fame 'as spread before you, young Arthur. Now listen, you go careful an' call for help should you need it. Use those gifts when the time arises. We be ready for the Call.'

'What call?'

'Don't you know?' He looked up and down the track before coming to a decision. 'Sorry lad, no time for that now, there be listenin' ears. Just remember what I say – we be ready.'

Arthur felt cold. A chill ran through him. It wasn't just the mist but a sense of danger creeping up on him.

'Ah, I see you be feelin' it too boy. Yes, I be thinkin' you be The One.'

'What d'you mean?' Arthur asked mystified.

'You'll know soon enough, boy.' Leaning down to stroke the dog, the man instructed, 'Keep watch, Lightning.' Then he raised his cap, smiled, and disappeared into the mist.

Puzzled, Arthur watched him go, yet he felt strangely comforted – which was bizarre because he had no idea who the stranger was and he still had that powerful sense of danger. It only occurred to him as he turned to continue up the path that he hadn't mentioned Lightning's name to anyone and yet the stranger had known it.

He walked on, wondering about the walker and the suggestion that he could call for help. It was probably his imagination but it was almost as if the man expected him to need help at some time.

Hope I don't! he thought. 'We're going to be all right, aren't we boy?'

Lightning's response was just a miserable whine.

So perhaps it was fortunate that Arthur was unaware that his progress was being monitored both from above and at ground level. Above him, a large, black bird circled and swooped in and out of the mist; while sometimes behind Arthur, and sometimes to his side, a sleek creature padded, occasionally glancing upwards with a growl whenever it caught sight of the bird.

Unaware and unappreciative of all this attention, Arthur looked on up the track. There, a little way off, was the entrance to the quarry. It was still as dark and forbidding as it had been only the other day, but to his relief he remembered that to get to where he was heading he didn't need to go right in.

He stopped and peered at the hillside beside him.

The other track was around here somewhere. Carefully staying on the path, he retraced his steps. Mossy and overgrown, but with some stones showing through the undergrowth, was a steep track leading down the hill.

Arthur took a deep breath and started to edge down the hillside. The path was steeper than it had first appeared and almost immediately he was slithering and slipping out of control. Desperately, he tried to keep his speed down. Suddenly the hill levelled out but by now he was running so fast that he cannoned into a high, stone wall. He shouted out as he hit the granite-hard stones, and his cry echoed across the hills, announcing his presence to anyone who might be interested. Lightning's arrival was more controlled, but with his tail hanging down and his ears flat against his head, he was quite clearly terrified.

Arthur crouched down and stroked him, 'It's okay, boy, there's nothing to be frightened of.'

But the dog whimpered, trembling from head to foot.

'Look,' Arthur said, trying to ignore the inner voice urging him to run, 'I'll be as quick as I can, then we'll go home.'

He straightened up, determined to find out whatever this place could tell him, and looked around. The wall he'd crashed into led away into the mist but there, to his left, was a high gate. He edged towards it through the dense undergrowth until he was close enough to examine it. For some reason, he was certain that this place held the key to some of the things that had been happening to him.

On either side of the rusted, wrought-iron gate there were two high, stone pillars. Topping each pillar was a carved statue. Arthur looked at them and then remembered what that new history teacher had said. She'd been teaching them about the ancient Assyrian empire. She'd said that people back then believed that a gateway could be a portal for good or evil, so they used to put carved statues either side of a gate in order to protect it. He also remembered how she'd looked at him when she'd said this. It was the sort of look that said, 'Remember this!'

He examined the carvings. One of them was a knight brandishing a sword, with a cloak flowing out behind him. The other statue held a shield and a short dagger. They were standing looking out over the moor as if they'd been frozen in time – a pair of ancient, mythical knights.

'I wonder if you guys have been able to protect this place!' he said. But looking at the brambles and weeds he doubted that anyone had been near it in years.

Then another thought struck him, 'Of course – the knight!'

He reached deep inside his pocket and found the model given to him by the shopkeeper in Pendrym. He looked at it carefully, checking every detail and matching it to the knight with the sword. It was exactly the same! But as he held it, something was happening.

The model was starting to glow and heat was spreading out from it.

And then he heard them.

He spun around – no one was there, but he was certain that he'd heard someone speaking. Snippets of conversation drifted towards him.

'The boy is there now!'

'How long has he been there?'

'He's just arrived.'

'So now we Watch. They will meet soon and another piece will be in place.'

The first voice started to reply but as it did so it faded away, leaving Arthur in silence with just Lightning for company. He looked at the model in his hand, it was cooling down. Arthur stood frozen, trying to make some sort of sense of all that had just happened but it was impossible; there was no way any of it could be explained.

Suddenly a shower of stones skittered down the hillside behind him. He turned quickly, his heart hammering in his chest, only to be confronted by a boy of about his age. With the blood pounding in his ears and his hand ready on the thread around his neck it slowly dawned on him that he'd seen this person before – and he wasn't any kind of a threat. It was the boy from the shop in Pendrym.

'Sorry about that. I didn't mean to make you jump.'

'Make me jump?' Arthur retorted angrily. 'I nearly had a heart attack! What do you think you're doing following me up here?' Then a thought struck him. 'Were you speaking to someone?'

The boy looked confused. 'Speaking to someone? No, I'm here by myself. Why, what did you hear?'

Arthur looked at him; he didn't feel like explaining what had happened to a total stranger. 'Never mind, perhaps you can tell me why you're here – and don't tell me it's a coincidence!'

'Um, well,' the boy started, 'it's a long story.'

'Go on,' replied Arthur furiously. 'I've got all the time in the world.'

'Well ... actually you haven't,' the boy said, looking around. 'That's part of the reason I'm here.'

'What are you on about? I've had enough of people talking in riddles; don't you start!'

The boy was about to say something but stopped and glanced at the sky.

'Look, there's no time for explanations now. You must trust me. You've got to get away from here.'

This was too much for Arthur and even though deep inside he knew the boy was right, a stubborn inner voice was protesting. Why should he be told what to do?

'Not until I've finished checking this place out.'

Arthur turned his back and started to examine the wall beside the gate. He'd had enough of people suggesting that he might be in danger. He was aware of that and he wasn't in the mood for more conversation. So he didn't notice the boy's desperate expression, or the way he quickly scanned the hill and the sky again. Neither did he hear him mumble something about inspecting the back of the house before disappearing.

There it was; he knew he'd been right.

Hidden under the creeping ivy was a name carved in granite set back in the wall. His fingers traced the lettering: 'Granite House – Arthur's Keep'. His name! Now he had to go through the gate. He had to find what secrets this place held. Pushing all negative thoughts away, he leant on the latch.

'Come on,' he urged. 'Open up.'

Years of neglect and rust had seized it solid, but Arthur was determined, he had to know what was behind the wall ... or in the house.

'No going back now,' he said stubbornly to himself, leaning all his weight on the gate. He gave a firm push with his shoulder and still it didn't move. Arthur was just beginning to think that he might have to give up after all when, with a reluctant groan, the gate finally gave way and creaked open. He'd done it! Black thoughts crowded his brain, warning him to go no further; but once again he pushed them away.

'Come on boy,' he said to the dog.

But Lightning refused to move. He raised his hackles and growled, standing between Arthur and the gate.

'Sorry boy, I've got to go in. You stay here. I'll be back in a minute. You can tell our new friend where I've gone.'

Arthur stepped past Lightning into a garden that hadn't been touched in years. Nettles grew to waist height, wild roses wound through crooked apple trees and brambles ran riot.

'Ow!' he muttered as thorns tore at his arms and legs. 'There'd better not be a Sleeping Beauty here – I'm not into kissing princesses.'

It was exactly like the setting for a fairy-tale. There was an air of desolation about the place, as if it hadn't been touched for decades, and the path was completely overgrown. A blackbird took flight with a squawk and there was a rustling in the undergrowth. Arthur started nervously and, glancing back over his shoulder, realised that there was no sign of Lightning.

Something didn't feel right. Although if he was honest with himself it had felt weird ever since he'd come down the path. Perhaps, he thought reluctantly, the dog and the boy had been right after all. He decided that he'd just have a very quick look so that at least he'd have followed up his idea, and then he could give himself permission to go - because with every step he took, his uneasiness grew.

He rounded a bend and there in front of him was an enormous house. Tall, granite walls topped by grey, slate roofs rose high above him. Leaded windows like unseeing eyes looked out and the only sound was the regular drip from the corroded guttering. Crows circled. He stepped back – he'd seen enough. A twig snapped behind him and he turned.

It was the Crow Man.

Chapter 15

Captive

For a brief moment the mist cleared and the sun broke through, casting shadows on the wall of the house. The Crow Man strode forward, thrust his arm around Arthur's neck and forced his head back. Arthur was dimly aware of a black shape wheeling in and out of the grey mist high above him. His captor's companion was making a victory fly-past.

His vision became cloudy as the pressure on his throat increased and, again it was as if he was outside himself, watching from somewhere far off. Could he see the boy and the dog outside the wall, or was that just wishful thinking?

Heart pounding and dry mouthed, he found himself being thrust forward, held in an iron grip. Arthur knew that even if he was given the opportunity to escape he wouldn't be able to run. And then he was being pushed through a gnarled and ancient oak door into the high-ceilinged hall of the Granite House. There was the sound of no return as the door clanged shut behind him and the bolts were hammered home.

He was in the house, in a hallway of dark, stone walls with a cold, slate floor. At the foot of the stairs a cobweb-covered suit of armour stood to attention with a fly hanging from the helmet, trapped in the spider's sticky threads. As Arthur was forced forward it felt as if, once again, unseen fingers were tugging and pinching him. He was living through a horror movie.

This can't be happening! he thought. But the stench from the Crow Man was real enough.

He was driven through a set of tall, arched doors leading off the hallway into a vast room. At the end of the room two winged chairs were placed either side of a granite fireplace. The fire was lit but it didn't give out any warmth, just burnt with an intense light. A dog lay in front of it, white from head to tail, but when it turned its eyes to Arthur he saw that they were pink, not brown like Lightning's eyes. The animal continued to gnaw the bone in front of him and watched Arthur impassively as saliva dripped onto the floor.

Arthur's captor propelled him further into the room, their footsteps echoing, and levered him into one of the winged chairs. As yet he hadn't seen anyone else but now he raised his eyes.

Sitting opposite him, dressed from head to foot in black, was probably the oldest woman he'd ever seen. Her yellow skin was stretched like parchment over her bones and thin, grey hair was scraped back from her face. Her nose was large and hooked and her mouth was little more than a slit. If she hadn't moved Arthur could have believed she was dead. He'd never understood what people meant by evil personified but he knew now; and it felt as though it was spreading out towards him.

'So, our visitor has arrived.' Her voice was a hiss. 'You have been long awaited.'

Arthur sat frozen by this new horror.

'Your name, sir.'

Arthur tried to speak but he couldn't find his voice.

She repeated tonelessly, 'Your name, sir.'

'Arthur,' he whispered.

'Your full birth name sir.'

Eventually he croaked, 'Arthur Penhaligon.'

He was shaking; shock was setting in.

There was silence, broken only by a crackle from the fire accompanied by smoke billowing into the room.

She looked at him. 'Ahh,' a breath escaping, 'it is as I thought. The One we have long awaited has come to us.'

Her tongue flicked out, her hands clutched the chair and smoke swirled around them. She leant forward, studying him intensely. His heart was racing, every beat thumping in his ears, while he shivered uncontrollably. Arthur tried to order his thoughts, to think over any clues he might have left behind about his intention to come to this house, but he'd said nothing to anyone. His mum would kill him. No one would have any idea he was here, except of course the boy and the dog.

Suddenly the silence in the great room was broken by a faint bleep dragging Arthur back to the reality he knew. Someone was texting him but he couldn't respond; his limbs were leaden and now the woman was alerted. She gestured with a nod of her head to the Crow Man standing behind him. He reached down to take the phone from Arthur's hand but, as he did, it broke into a melody and the Crow Man leapt back as if he'd been bitten. The tune continued for a few seconds more and then stopped.

Little by little an idea was taking shape through the fog that had been clouding Arthur's mind. He realised that these people had probably never used, or perhaps even encountered, a mobile phone. There was no way he could use it now but maybe he could call or text someone – if he chose his moment carefully. Gradually, despite his perilous situation, his mind was clearing.

The woman was leaning forward, her tongue licking her lips. He had to act quickly before they took away his lifeline.

'Er, it's a toy,' he gabbled, finding his voice and thinking as rapidly as he could. 'And sometimes it just goes off.'

He carried on, 'I'll put it in my pocket.'

Slowly, he transferred it to his jacket pocket and let his hand rest there while he held his breath. The woman continued to scrutinise his face, her eyes unblinking.

'We don't like music,' she hissed. 'Silence is all that is needed.'

But she didn't motion to the Crow Man and neither did he move forward. There was silence until suddenly, and with startling ease, she hauled herself out of the chair. She was both taller and stronger than Arthur had expected. She lunged forward and seized a sword hanging on the wall next to a shield. In one swift movement she turned and lifted the weapon above her head before swinging it down, missing Arthur's ear by a hair's breadth.

He flinched, terrified.

Gripping the sword in one hand, she bent over him until her nose almost touched his; flecks of saliva clung to her lips. She grasped his face, digging her fingernails into his skin.

'That is the only music we need – metal cutting air … or flesh.'

For a long minute she held him until eventually, satisfied that she'd asserted her authority, she released him and replaced the weapon on the wall. Unmoved by the actions of its mistress the dog continued to crush the bone.

Arthur shook. Blood oozed from his face where her fingernails had penetrated. He now knew for certain that these people were both dangerous and mad.

At that moment a shout echoed from a room somewhere deep in the house and, for the first time since he'd been forced into this place, Arthur felt the woman's attention distracted from him as her eyes shifted towards the door. For a second she seemed to hesitate before gesticulating impatiently towards the Crow Man saying, 'Go – fetch him.'

The Crow Man disappeared and she turned back to Arthur. 'There is someone here who also has been waiting for you. He is deluded, a fool, as you will see for yourself.'

The woman's eyes flicked back towards his pocket. She was still suspicious and he knew that at any minute she could choose to take his phone from him; he had to divert her attention.

Summoning all his energy, he asked the first thing that came into his head. 'Why've you been waiting for me? I'm not important am I?'

Her reaction astonished him. 'Ha!' she spat, and her gnarled hands reached up to her withered neck. 'You – not important?'

She dragged something out which was hanging from a chain around her neck. It looked like a miniature sword. It was carved from the same stone that had been left by the Crow Man in his kitchen.

'Your name is Arthur Penhaligon.'

Arthur gazed at her.

'I still don't get it,' he said, desperate to keep her talking but also because he really *didn't* get it.

'You belong with us. It was always your destiny to come to us.'

'But what's a sword got to do with anything?' he asked, emboldened. A part of him was genuinely interested.

'They haven't told you?'

'No one's said anything,' Arthur said, thinking that it would have helped if someone had told him something. At least then he might have been better prepared for all of this. 'And,' he muttered, 'I don't know who "they" are.'

But the woman's attention was wavering and she sighed as if she'd already had enough of this short conversation.

'If it's my destiny to come here, what am I supposed to do?' he persisted, determined to know at least a little more.

However, she simply looked at him, her hooded eyes blinking, and said, 'That will be shown to you at the appointed time.'

There was a movement in the doorway and two people appeared. One was the Crow Man but the other was a man virtually bent in two. Arthur was amazed that he was able to walk. This man shuffled closer then stopped and turned to fix Arthur with unseeing eyes. Arthur had thought the woman was the oldest person he'd ever met, but this man was far, far older. He had white, matted hair and a beard that reached down to his knees while his eyes were a blind, milky white.

'Sire.' A single word.

'Fool!' the woman spat. 'Who are you naming? Your blindness has made you more feeble-minded.'

She strode across, raising her hand to strike him, but he continued, 'Blind of eye I may be, Matearnas, but my spirit sings.'

'You know nothing. You see nothing. He is but a boy.'

'A boy perhaps – but one with a destiny!'

Throughout this exchange Arthur hardly registered what was being said but instead was marvelling at the whole appearance of the newcomer, especially his clothes. They reminded him of the model Great-Uncle Lance had given him.

'Ah, but not all destinies are fulfilled.'

'Nothing will stand in the way of this one. Even you will find your wish, your desire, bent to one stronger than you.'

'I think not. I have made preparations.'

With that she pointed to a glass, and the Crow Man left the side of the wizened man and approached a heavily carved table where a cut-glass bottle, its facets dulled by dust, sat waiting. In the bottle a liquid was swirling and bubbling, its colour constantly changing from brown to purple to murky green. The Crow Man filled the long-stemmed glass with the liquid and then turned and, advancing towards Arthur, held it out for him to take. Arthur's stomach heaved. There was no way he could drink that!

And then there was a sound, so faint as to be almost inaudible, on the extreme limit of his hearing. The dog heard it too and, with his ears pricked and the bone forgotten, he stood up and howled. The sound grew stronger. It sounded like singing.

The woman shrank back, looking around and above her, fear etched across her face. And the glass being offered to Arthur shattered from rim to stem, spilling the liquid, which oozed and splashed steaming onto the floor, sizzling as it met the cold, stone surface. A warm glow swept from Arthur's fingers to the tips of his toes and absurdly he thought, *Better out than in!*

He'd heard that sound before – at the Jollys' house.

Chapter 16

Escape?

As the singing died away the light that had suffused the room faded, and darkness once again unfurled, reaching out from the corners and recesses towards Arthur. A silence descended, broken only by the occasional hiss and bubble at Arthur's feet as the liquid from the glass settled and evaporated. The dog sat panting. Both the Crow Man and the woman had their eyes firmly fixed on him, but the old man was gazing upwards with just a hint of a smile.

'How long have I waited to hear that song?' he murmured to himself.

Amazed at all that had happened and seemingly on his behalf, Arthur sat stupefied.

Just as well, I didn't have that drink, he thought, watching the last of the foaming liquid seep away. *Looks like it could have done some damage.*

Suddenly the woman appeared to come to a decision. 'It appears that you are of interest to others,' she murmured thoughtfully. 'Perhaps it is time for you to be told.'

She paused dramatically and her eyes became distant. She stood with her arms hanging straight, seeming more than ever like an ancient mummy. Looking at Arthur, as if checking that she had his full attention, she raised her head and started to speak.

'I am Matearnas, queen of this place. I am queen of these moors, of Cornwall and everything above and below it. There are others that would have you as king, the Guardian, of this land but they will soon find that they have long been deceived.'

Arthur was dumbfounded. She was deadly serious.

Having made her announcement, Matearnas signalled to the Crow Man and Arthur was wrenched from the chair.

'Time, I think, to fulfil our destiny.' She turned and spoke to Arthur's captor: 'You have all we need?'

The Crow Man inclined his head, saying nothing. Matearnas nodded and without a sound she glided ahead of them, her dog at her side. The group, with Matearnas taking the lead, made their way outside – the old, wooden door crashing shut behind them.

***

Although he was still a prisoner, Arthur felt tremendous relief at being out in the damp, grey air. Here at least he could shout and someone might hear him; but then he looked around and his heart sank, because the light was already fading. How many hours had passed since he'd been captured? It didn't seem possible, but he must have been in the house far longer than he'd realised. Furthermore the mist was thick, adding to the gloom; sensible people don't go for walks in the mist.

'Fetch the mount, we must make speed,' she demanded.

Turning to the ancient man she continued, 'Bedivere, you will be reunited with your horse for this, your last, journey. You are to be witness to all that will unfold.'

That name – why was it familiar? Arthur combed his memory, searching for the link.

'Matearnas, even now you can choose a different path,' Bedivere replied. But any further conversation was halted by the reappearance of the Crow Man leading a horse as aged as the rest of the company.

'Ah, my old friend,' Bedivere whispered, shuffling forward. 'I never thought to meet you again.'

He held his hands out in front of him, feeling his way to the horse's head and softly stroked its mane.

'Have we come to this, you and I?'

The horse nickered softly in reply, pawing the ground, and nuzzled the old man. For a moment Arthur forgot all that was happening to him, he was so caught up in the emotion of the two old friends meeting up after who knew how long.

'Enough!' Matearnas commanded, looking at the sky. 'There is no more time.'

She nodded towards Arthur. 'Quickly, tie his arms and keep him close.'

Arthur's arms were twisted behind his back and tied, the rope cutting into his skin. There was no chance now of reaching his phone – or the whistle, which at last, with a sinking heart, he remembered. The ancient man was levered up onto his mount and the group set out, driven on by the woman.

Incredibly for someone of Matearnas's age, she walked so fast that she made it almost impossible for Arthur to keep up. The Crow Man held him by the shoulder, his fingers digging into Arthur's flesh, driving him relentlessly forward. Brambles tore at Arthur's face and clothes as Matearnas led the small group towards the quarry, following the same path he'd come along earlier.

Then, out of the corner of his eye, something caught

Arthur's attention. He looked again and saw a shape moving through the mist alongside them. As he was propelled forward he risked a longer look.

Prowling to his side a large, black shape padded silently, mist swirling around it. There was a blink of a wide, green eye and then, unbelievably, a rough tongue and a warm breath on his hand and a deep, rumbling purr. The creature moved forward to walk beside the horse and its master. The horse didn't start but just glanced sideways. It seemed to Arthur that, as he watched, it became stronger. Not only that, but Bedivere was becoming straighter and taller in the saddle. Then with a flick of a long, black tail, and as quickly as it had appeared, the animal was gone.

It could have been coincidence, but at precisely that instant the Crow Man skidded on the mossy path and, losing his footing, released Arthur from his hold. Arthur stumbled, trying to make sense of all he'd just witnessed when he realised that here, at last, was his chance.

Slithering over the wet grass and clambering over the boulders that littered his route, he staggered and slid; desperate to escape his living nightmare.

Every step was an effort. Running with his arms lashed behind his back was almost impossible. He ran as fast as he could but his lack of balance and the treacherous conditions worked against him. Weaving between brambles and mossy rocks and hawthorn trees, he didn't dare look over his shoulder. Didn't dare see how much distance he'd put between him and his abductor. Any moment and the Crow Man's hand could imprison him. Then, quite suddenly, his foot slipped deep into a hidden rabbit hole and with a sickening jolt he lurched sideways. He was unable to save himself and pitched towards the ground, landing with a bone-jarring thud.

Jagged pain shot from his ankle to his knee and the metallic taste of blood filled his mouth. The phone flew out of his pocket and smashed against a boulder and despair filled him. He'd blown his escape.

Then someone called his name. 'Arthur!'

He lay still, numbed by the fall, incapable of responding.

'Art, over here.'

Groaning, he tried to move.

'Art, there's not much time,' the voice continued insistently. 'Quickly, look over here!'

Slowly and painfully he turned his head, blearily peering through the shadows. The mist had thinned enough to make out the figure of a boy, or young man, standing a little way from him.

'Listen Art, you're going to be all right but you must do whatever Bedivere advises you. Never doubt him.'

But all Arthur thought was, *The only one who ever called me 'Art' was Great-Uncle Lance.*

At that point the stranger glanced back along the path and, just as Arthur was about to summon the strength to speak, mist swirled between them ... and when it cleared there was no sign of Arthur's ally – just Matearnas's dog charging towards him.

Arthur flinched, slamming his eyes closed, but there was a yelp and a whimper and when he looked again he saw the hound frozen, its eyes focused to the left of his shoulder. It started to whine and back away, its ears flat and its tail between its legs.

For a split second he was sure that he'd heard a deep-throated growl but before he had time to look around the Crow Man was upon him. His keeper seized his bound arms and heaved him to his feet, stretching every ligament; and Arthur cried out as a searing pain shot through his ankle. Blood trickled from his nose and a gash on his forehead, and the wounds on his legs oozed and stung. With a grunt his captor pushed him forward but this time he held him even more tightly. There wasn't going to be a second chance.

But something positive had come out of his attempt to escape because the rope around his arms had definitely loosened. So, trying to block the stabbing pain shooting from his ankle and the blood seeping into his eyes, Arthur started to work at the knot on his wrist. However, Matearnas was beside herself with fury. Her captive had tried to escape! Spinning around she grabbed Arthur's hair and wrenched his head back until he was looking up into her eyes.

'Never attempt to escape again,' she spat at him. 'Understand this; you are coming with us – dead or alive.'

The Crow Man tugged harshly at Arthur's arms making him cry out. Speaking for the first time, he growled in his ear, 'Better believe it, boy.'

Then turning on her heel, Matearnas led the group deeper into the moors and further away from civilisation. By-passing the quarry they walked on. The sky was darkening but the mist had begun to clear, blown away by a light breeze.

'Where are we going?' Arthur asked, his voice barely a whisper.

The Crow Man looked down at him impassively but said nothing, just gripped him more tightly and pushed him stumbling forward.

Matearnas slowed down and turned to face him. 'Understand this, Arthur Penhaligon; it is of little use trying to escape. Your destiny is to be with us.'

She said this so quietly he was chilled. Her indifference was far more terrifying than her anger.

'But where are we going?' Arthur persisted, desperation giving him a voice. 'There's nothing out here.'

The woman merely looked at him and he was once again given the impression that he was nothing more than an object to her.

'You will find out soon enough.'

And with these words she continued to lead the little procession deeper into the moors.

Chapter 17

The summons

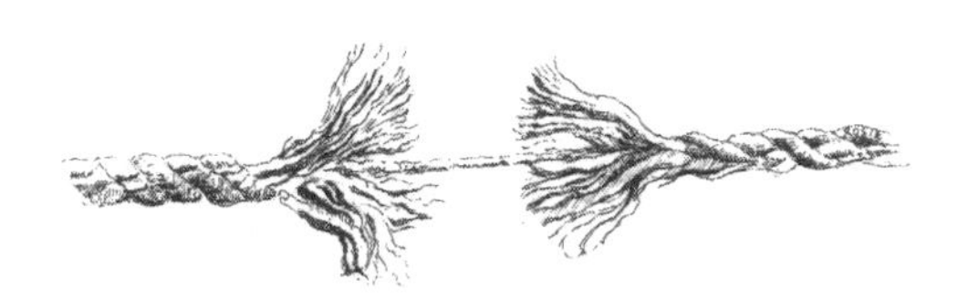

The path turned, climbing steeply up the side of a tor, and Arthur found himself walking beside the horse and its master. Blotting out the pain, he tried to organise his thoughts. Who was the stranger who'd appeared after he'd fallen, and how did he know both Arthur and Bedivere?

And that name, it was familiar. Then it came to him – 'Bedivere', of course! That must be the faded inscription on the model that he'd been given by his great-uncle. Hadn't he been one of the knights in the court of King Arthur? No, that was impossible!

The old man was now sitting straight and had also, it seemed, recovered his sight because he was looking Arthur straight in the eye.

He leant towards him with obvious concern. 'Sire, you are wounded.'

Arthur cast a cautionary look towards Matearnas ahead of them, and over his shoulder to the Crow Man. He was a few paces behind.

'I'm okay. I don't think anything's broken.'

Keeping his voice low so as not to let the Crow Man hear, he asked, 'Do you know him then?'

Bedivere looked puzzled.

'You must know him,' Arthur continued quietly. The Crow Man pushed him. He stumbled.

Bedivere waited until there was space between them and their captor, and lowered his voice. 'To whom do you refer, sire?'

Dropping his voice to a whisper to avoid angering the Crow Man, Arthur said, 'That guy back there; he seemed to know you and he knew my name – he called me "Art".'

At this Bedivere swung round to face him. 'Who did you see?'

'I told you,' Arthur whispered. 'A boy or a man. It was difficult to see him but I'm sure I've never met him.'

Bedivere glanced at the Crow Man before asking, 'What did he call you?'

'I told you – "Art".'

'And he knew me by name?'

Arthur was beginning to lose patience.

'Yes – and,' he said remembering, 'he told me to do whatever you told me to, or something like that.'

Bedivere's reaction took Arthur completely by surprise. Throwing his head back he laughed out loud ignoring any threat from their captors. Arthur cast a nervous glance towards Matearnas but fortunately she was way ahead, totally wrapped up in her mission and perhaps, for now at least, the Crow Man's sole intention seemed to be to keep him moving.

'You've seen him then.' Bedivere stated in an undertone but with an enormous smile. 'I was right: you are The One.'

Arthur ignored this statement. 'But who is he?'

'It would take too long to make everything clear to you sire – the time will come, but it is not now.'

Arthur was becoming increasingly annoyed with this response. Wouldn't anyone answer his questions? He glanced forward at the woman to check that it was still safe to talk.

Then he whispered, 'Okay, but there's something I would like to know: you can't be the Bedivere who was one of King Arthur's knights.'

'Is that a statement or a question, sire?' Bedivere asked quietly.

Arthur thought for a few seconds. 'Both, I suppose.'

For a while the only response he got was silence, until Bedivere replied softly, 'There are more things under the heavens than we can ever imagine, sire.'

'But I …' Arthur was lost for words as he tried to absorb the implications of this answer. And then another thought struck him. Whispering again, he asked, 'Why do you keep calling me that?'

With a low chuckle Bedivere said, 'All will become clear at the appointed time … sire.'

Then, raising an eyebrow, he nodded towards Matearnas and darted a quick look over his shoulder at the Crow Man, indicating that all conversation should cease.

'I don't understand any of this and you still haven't answered my question!'

'Enough for the moment,' Bedivere replied. In little more than a murmur, he added, 'Concentrate instead on attaining your freedom.'

'What do you think I've been doing?' Arthur said hotly.

A second chuckle. 'Aye, like my Lord in manner too.'

However, before he had time to ask Bedivere another question, the Crow Man shoved Arthur between his shoulder blades, sending him stumbling towards an immense building resembling a tall, roofless house with ivy clinging to its walls. An enormous, cylindrical chimney stood to the side. This was a disused mine, last used many decades ago.

A fire had been lit at the base of the tower; the flames licked the wall and showers of sparks flew out. The Crow

Man thrust Arthur towards the fire where Matearnas was waiting for him with her dog at her side. Arthur continued walking, urged on by his minder, until an agonising pain brought him to his senses and he was jerked to a halt.

His eyes began to adjust to his surroundings. A large hollow lay between him and the woman, but as he walked closer to the fire the flickering light illuminated it, showing deeper, darker depths. It was one of the old mine shafts reaching deep into the ground.

Matearnas had started to speak. 'Arthur Penhaligon, you may be the appointed Guardian of our land but I now claim the royal heritage.'

Foreboding filled him. But, at that moment, Bedivere's voice rang out. He'd turned to Arthur and was shouting at him – 'Now sire, summon them now!'

For some seconds Arthur stood paralysed, and then a memory jabbed its finger sharply into his mind. Of course, the whistle! He tugged at the rope binding his wrists. Simultaneously, Matearnas strode towards him and the Crow Man reached down, but with a final tug the rope gave way. And at last, wrenching the thread from around his neck, Arthur pulled out the whistle and blew.

Immediately Matearnas was crying out and clasping her hands to her ears as she tried to shut out the sound. The Crow Man did the same, momentarily freeing Arthur – only to stagger behind him and send him lurching forward, perilously close to the edge of the chasm.

Arms flailing, Arthur swayed, desperately trying to regain his balance - and someone screamed his name.

Chapter 18

All for one

From the moment she'd woken up Tamar had been anxious. It was a nagging worry, one of those that wasn't about anything in particular but just wouldn't go away. It felt a bit like waking up on the morning of an exam when she hadn't done enough revision. And she knew it was to do with Arthur.

She'd tried to distract herself by listening to her sister talking on the phone to a friend; something about a boy. It was always about a boy. Tamar wondered which one Morwenna had in mind this time. She almost felt sorry for him. She'd wandered around Morwenna's room, fiddling with her make-up and leafing through her magazines until her sister had found her.

'You know you're not allowed in here!' Morwenna had shouted. 'Put that down ...'

'Okay, okay!' Tamar retorted. 'I'm going.'

The door slammed behind her and she heard Morwenna quickly in conversation with another of her friends complaining about Tamar, before launching into further discussion about the boy. So Tamar had drifted back to her own room and slumped onto her bed.

She'd tried to reason that there was nothing to worry about but, try as she might, she couldn't shift the sickening sensation that something terrible was about to happen.

She sat in her room discussing her concerns with Mug Shot but he didn't give her any answers. 'You know, you're not being any help at all,' she told him.

Mug Shot wagged his tail and rolled over.

'D'you think I should phone Arthur?' she asked.

She picked up her phone, but sat undecided for several minutes. Tamar hated people who fussed and that was exactly what she was about to do. But the feeling that Arthur was in trouble was growing, gnawing away at her. She would just have to swallow her pride and phone him. At least then she'd know he was all right.

'Right, here goes!' she announced, scrolling to his name.

But Arthur didn't answer; instead she listened to the recording asking her to leave a message. She remembered Arthur making it while Nick fooled about, trying to put him off. If you listened carefully you could hear their giggles in the background.

'This is ridiculous!' she said to herself. Mug Shot wagged his tail in agreement. 'I'm sure I'm getting wound up over nothing.'

But however calm she tried to be she couldn't banish the sense of something being wrong … she'd just have to phone Nick and put up with him teasing her. It would be worth it to know that Arthur was okay. She didn't care if he thought that she was being stupid.

'Hiya,' she began, casually. 'Have you heard from Arthur today?'

'Nope,' Nick yawned. 'Not today. He was still going on about the moors last night – maybe he's gone back up there.'

'Why on earth would he do that!' she exclaimed.

Nick glanced at the phone in his hand. Tamar was unusually wound up.

'I mean,' she continued, trying to sound more reasonable, 'why would he go up there after what happened last time?'

'To be honest, I haven't thought about it.'

'Didn't you try and put him off going back?'

'He's old enough to make his own decisions and he still has that dog – he told me that his parents were leaving it till today to find the owners – so I figured he'd be fine. Anyway you know Arthur when he's got an idea ...' Nick trailed off.

Tamar was beginning to feel that maybe she was right to be worried. 'Do his folks know?'

'I don't think so.' Nick ran over their conversation. 'No, I'm pretty sure they don't. I don't even *know* myself – I'm only guessing.'

Tamar chewed a nail. 'Listen Nick, this may sound a bit strange – but I'm sure he's in trouble.'

'Why?'

'Just because ... oh, I don't know.' She sighed. 'It's just one of those weird feelings. Don't you ever get them?'

There was silence at the other end of the phone. She could picture the puzzled look on Nick's face so she ploughed on. 'Look, he's not replied to any of my texts and he's normally good at that ... even if you're not!'

'Yeah,' Nick conceded. 'You've got a point there, and I'll ignore the insult.'

'Seriously Nick, I've got the feeling that something's wrong.'

Tamar's anxiety was infectious. She could be right. Perhaps Arthur was in some sort of danger and they should get up to the moors ... maybe he should have found out more from Arthur about what his plans were – and put him off going up to the moors by himself.

'Have you still got your bike?' he suddenly asked her.

'Yeah, I haven't used it for a while, but it's still in the back of the shed. Why?'

'Well, *if* he's gone up there, it's going to be our best way of following him; there's not a bus for ages. How about if we meet up in ten minutes? The Corner Shop's the best place – it's almost on Moor Road.'

Tamar was so relieved to be finally doing something that she didn't hesitate for a minute. 'I'll be there.'

Jamming his phone into his pocket, Nick leapt down the stairs. By now it was the afternoon and Tamar was right, Arthur nearly always phoned or texted back promptly. A long silence like this was totally out of character.

Minutes later, as he cycled along the road, Nick looked at the mist. He could barely see more than a few metres ahead. *And,* he thought grimly, *it'll be even thicker higher up.*

***

The street cleaner leant on his broom and Watched Nick cycle into the mist.

He spoke to his companion. 'So, the boy's friends are on their way.'

'Does the Writer know?'

Viatoris nodded. 'She said that we must wait and Watch until we hear the Call and then we may go. Cathe is up there, and Argo is ready.'

He looked at Servo's feet, still in old, leather sandals. The other Watcher, catching the look stated, 'It is difficult – having to Watch in two places and in two such different times!'

The street cleaner smiled. 'I imagine it must be, Servo. How is the boy in Egypt?'

A note of pride crept into the Watcher's voice, 'He does well! He is so young but already trusted by those in high places.'

Both Watchers were silent, one considering a boy in far-off times and in a far-away place; the other thinking of a boy far closer with an equally intriguing destiny.

***

Nick and Tamar rode out of town towards the country. Their friendship may be punctuated with arguments, but today Tamar was very happy to see Nick.

They approached the hills, pedalling hard, all the time deep in discussion about what would be their best approach to finding Arthur.

'I think we should go and ask Michael and Angela for help,' Tamar suggested. 'It's no good us two rushing around in this mist.'

Nick agreed, 'Yeah, I was beginning to think that too.'

They knew that it might have been sensible to ring Arthur's parents, but they both had a feeling that there were other adults who would be more helpful. They'd already dismissed the idea of asking the police – someone a bit more *special* was needed.

They were silent, contemplating the size of the moors and the forbidding landscape ... and the diminishing light. It was much later than either of them would have liked.

'Is it okay,' Tamar began, 'if we go straight to the Jollys' cottage?'

'Definitely,' Nick agreed. 'Anything else would be stupid.'

Tamar carried on, 'It's odd isn't it?

'What is?'

'How we hardly know Michael and Angela ... but they're the people we trust most.'

Nick swerved to avoid a pothole and nodded, but didn't say anything. He had a gnawing feeling that every minute was vital - and all his energy was needed for propelling himself up the hills.

They cycled on in silence, until they finally reached the edge of the moors and more level ground, at last juddering over the cattle grid. They were oblivious to the large ginger cat monitoring their progress from the top of a dry-stone wall; however, the instant they were off the road, and onto the moor, they felt a deep rumbling which sounded – and felt – like far off thunder.

'What's that?' Tamar asked.

'Search me.'

They slid off their bikes and peered into the gloom, trying to see where the vibrations were coming from. The thudding came closer, then the mist eddied and parted to reveal a herd of wild, moorland ponies charging directly towards them.

'Nick!' Tamar screamed, grabbing his arm. (She'd be embarrassed about this later.)

'Stop!' Nick yelled helplessly, but the galloping hooves drowned him out.

At the very last minute, when it seemed certain that they must be trampled, the ponies veered and slowed from a gallop to a canter to a trot and then a walk. Whinnying and neighing and tossing their heads, they quietly encircled the youngsters and their bikes. There were snorts and more whinnies and a white stallion approached Tamar. First he nuzzled her face, snorting softly and then gave a low snicker, before turning and walking away.

For a good few moments neither Nick nor Tamar moved. They stood frozen, their hearts still racing.

Eventually Nick tore his gaze from the ponies and looked at Tamar. 'What's this all about?'

'It must be something to do with Arthur. There can't be any other explanation.'

The animals had formed a phalanx on either side of them, with the stallion at the head, and had begun to walk forward – Tamar and Nick were being escorted. They exchanged glances and heaved their bikes up.

'It's like having our very own security company,' Nick observed.

'Our very own *equine* security company! This is getting really, really weird.'

Nick, for once, was serious and nodded. 'But let's be honest, things have been strange for quite a while.'

Glancing at their escorts and casting her mind back over recent events, Tamar silently agreed.

The cottage came into sight, just visible through the low light and the mist, and their companions slowed and stood waiting, ensuring that their charges reached their destination safely. The stallion stood to one side, allowing them through to the cottage gate.

'Well, if it isn't Tamar and Nick!' Angela said, as she opened the door to their knocks.

Tamar heaved a sigh of relief and, without even bothering with a 'hello', plunged in. 'I'm so glad to see you Angela! We think Arthur's in trouble.'

Angela's expression changed as she looked at them and their escorts. 'You'd better come in and tell us about it.' She stood aside to let them into her sitting room before facing the assembled ponies. 'So, you were sent. Thank you my friends, a duty honourably discharged. You may go now, with our thanks.'

There were responding neighs and whinnies before the herd turned and galloped off across the moors leaving the stallion standing alone.

'As ever, a worthy commander, Argo,' Angela paused and added, 'T'is more than likely that you'll be needed again; be ready.'

The stallion pawed the ground and then it too swung around and thundered off.

***

Tamar and Nick entered the cottage's sitting room and saw Michael watching them from the fire-side chair. He looked anything but relaxed, and as they outlined the recent events – and their worries for Arthur, Michael's face mirrored their own concerns.

'So, we've tried texting him but he hasn't got back to us.'

'And he's usually good about that,' Tamar added, casting a meaningful look in Nick's direction.

'We think he wanted to get to the bottom of all the stuff that's been happening to him, especially with the Crow Man,' Nick said, ignoring Tamar's glance.

'Crow Man?' interjected Michael.

'You know – that weird guy who was up here last time.'

As soon as the Crow Man was mentioned the expressions on the Jollys' faces said it all and Michael got up and looked out of the window.

'Light's nearly gone, but it'll be a clear moon,' he observed, glancing up at the sky. 'Mist 'as cleared. T'is time to be going – there's not a moment to lose.'

While saying this he was collecting his hat and his crook. Calling his dog, he commanded, 'Come Fly.'

Tamar looked at the sky. It *was* late. If only she'd phoned Nick earlier; they'd wasted hours and hours of daylight. But before she had time to dwell on her thoughts she was being steered back outside. They were obviously going to be helping Michael in the search.

'Think you'd better be stayin' here m'dear,' he said to Angela.

He turned to Nick and Tamar and asked, 'What about Arthur's parents?'

Tamar and Nick exchanged a guilty look. Perhaps they *should* have phoned them already.

'Now don't you be worrying,' Angela cut in. 'I'll take care of that when the time arises. You must be going.'

Chapter 19

The search

Michael set off at a brisk pace with Nick and Tamar jogging at his side. Once again they found themselves following the path to the quarry. Neither of them talked but just concentrated on keeping up and watching the ground in front of them. They knew that without Michael guiding them they would have been hopelessly lost; especially with the light fading.

Then, in the distance, a figure emerged from the shadows –with a dog at its side.

'Arthur?' Tamar shouted.

But there was no answer; the person was too far away.

Nick peered into the dusk. 'I don't think it's him … but that looks like the dog we picked up yesterday.'

As their paths converged the dog raced ahead to meet them.

'Yeah, it's definitely the dog that came home with us.'

'What's it doing out here?'

Nick glanced over to Tamar. 'It must have come out with Arthur.'

'So where's Arthur?' Tamar asked.

By now they'd drawn level with a boy of about their age. He'd obviously been running and was panting and gripping his side, his jeans torn and blood stained.

'Ah, so it's you Gawain,' Michael stated.

The boy frowned, momentarily confused, but then his face cleared. 'You're one of Uncle's friends!'

Michael smiled briefly, 'I am indeed.' The smile disappeared. 'But I take it that you 'ave news for us.'

Gawain nodded before casting a look towards Tamar and Nick. He recognised them from when they'd come into the shop. For a moment nothing was said while they assessed one another.

Then a thought struck Tamar. 'How did you get Arthur's dog?'

'It's a bit of a long story. I'll tell you about it later.'

Nick and Tamar glanced at one another. It looked like Arthur really was in trouble.

Pushing his fingers through his dishevelled hair, the boy turned back to Michael. 'We've got to find them quickly.'

'Them?' Michael questioned.

'Yes, I think a man and a woman have got him.'

Michael, looking grave, muttered something quietly about Matearnas and her accomplice.

'I was trying to get him away,' Gawain continued, 'but a man caught him and took him into the house.'

'Arthur's Keep? The Granite House?'

'Yes, I think they'd been waiting for him.'

Michael said nothing but stood looking at the ground, deep in thought. Then he considered the darkening sky, a few stars just becoming visible against the deepening blue, and as if responding to an internal conversation, said, 'Yes, we know 'ow this is meant to be. But there's one who'll be there for 'im; he's in safe hands.'

With that he set off without another word. The three youngsters cast glances at each other and followed him.

No one talked. From time to time Tamar and Nick would look at one another, trying to reassure themselves that somewhere their world still existed. That in Lyskeret town far below them, ordinary people were still doing ordinary things: watching television, eating their tea or just playing computer games.

Tamar looked curiously at Gawain. He appeared to be about their age but somehow seemed older. She wondered how he'd come to be involved in all of this. But as Gawain had implied, there was no time for questions.

Michael continued striding out, past the quarry and on deeper into the moors, while both dogs ran ahead of the search party with their noses to the ground. A tight unit of canine search and rescue. They carried on in silence in case it disturbed Michael's concentration because it was as if he was listening to something; as if he had an inner transmitter tuned in for Arthur. From time to time he'd stop and look up into the sky and concentrate, frowning, and then with a nod he'd take off again.

They walked and jogged for what seemed like hours, negotiating the marshes and boulders that littered their way, but nobody complained or asked Michael to slow down. Instinctively they understood that this could be a matter of life or death.

***

It was Michael who saw the fire first, a beacon in the surrounding darkness. He grunted, 'That's Matearnas I reckon; she loves 'er fires.'

While they walked towards the light Michael talked quietly to them, explaining that it was imperative that they stay out of sight when they neared Arthur and his captors.

'She's an unsteady one and if you show yourselves it could be dangerous for Arthur, but do as I say and we'll 'ave him out of there safe and sound.'

It was at that moment that Arthur blew the whistle.

The air rippled and shivered. If circumstances had been different they might have noticed the stars shimmer and the dark blue of the sky putting on a light show of breathtaking beauty.

Instead they were transfixed by what followed.

As if in slow motion, they saw Arthur flail and teeter on the edge of the mine shaft, terrifyingly close to the yawning hole.

Instinctively Tamar cried out, screaming, 'Arthur!'

She stood frozen, her hands over her mouth and her eyes fixed on the tableau in front of her. But Michael just motioned to them to stay where they were and walked quietly forward, briefly resting his hand on Tamar's head as he passed. Strolling past Bedivere he whispered something and the old knight nodded, and slowly swung his horse towards the three youngsters.

By now Arthur was gripping a thorn bush on the very edge of the shaft, completely unable to move. Fear had overtaken every part of his body and mind. It would take only the smallest slip to send him hurtling into the depths of the mine.

Michael started to speak. 'Matearnas, clowas, convethas, (*hear, understand*) you know full well this boy's destiny. You cannot change what 'as been determined for 'im. Remember, every hair on that boy's head is special.'

The woman shrieked back at him, 'Me ore hedna per thaa. Voyd alebma!' (*I know that very well. Go away!*)

Michael paused before replying, his voice filling the air around them. 'Matearnas, if you know that to be the truth, you be knowin' the cost if you carry on.'

A flash of lightning coursed across the sky, illuminating Matearnas and Michael. He appeared far taller, a titan not a man. A wind whipped up, blasting the moors, bending trees, but he sauntered towards Arthur as if he was out for a Sunday afternoon stroll, all the time calmly talking to the woman.

'Matearnas, you know the good and right thing to do. Forget all that is past – there is still time for you to change.'

Thunder boomed overhead, shaking the ground.

By now Michael was almost with Arthur.

She spat back furiously, 'Never, Michael. Why would I want to change? Leave us.'

Michael was leaning over and saying something quietly to Arthur; then he reached out and pulled him up and away from the edge of the mine shaft. In that split second another flash of lightning lit the figures: the giant and the boy.

Michael turned to the woman and holding Arthur tightly, protecting him from any further harm, shouted into the wind.

'Matearnas, t'is time for you to make your choice. This boy may be a Guardian, but not for you and your kind. Which way will you go?'

The woman hissed, 'Never yours Michael. I am the queen of this place. And that boy,' she pointed a skeletal finger at Arthur, 'he is mine. He must stay with me. He will bow before me.'

She made as if to lunge towards Arthur, her hands outstretched, trying to pluck him from Michael's grasp, but as she did so a single white owl flew overhead. She flinched, holding her hand above her head as if to ward it off. She turned and staggered as a sleek, black shape emerged from the shadows. It advanced on her and Matearnas catching sight of it screamed, 'Not that Michael! Not that!'

She backed away.

The beast advanced and she spun around, desperate to escape, and scrambled onto a ledge jutting out high above the hillside. That side of the engine house fell steeply to a carpet of granite boulders below, so she didn't stand a chance, especially a woman of her age.

She glanced behind her. Any escape route was cut off – there was only one way out. A sickening realisation began to grip Tamar and Nick. Matearnas was going to jump. They couldn't believe what was about to happen but, even as they watched, she appeared to come to a decision. With her arms outstretched she stood at the edge of the ledge and then, very deliberately, toppled forward and fell, her body bouncing from boulder to boulder, her fragile bones splintering.

They would never forget that final, terrible scream. It was the scream of someone who'd chosen the dark path.

Chapter 20

Reunited

Tamar and Nick were mesmerised by Matearnas's fall, frozen by the horror of what they'd witnessed. So they didn't notice the quiet conversation between Bedivere and Gawain, and the ease with which they spoke to one another. And although perhaps, somewhere at the very back of their minds, they had registered Bedivere's unusual appearance, somehow it just didn't seem that important after all they'd experienced.

Nor did they notice the sudden quietening of the storm as the thunder and the wind died away to be replaced by a brilliant moon and a sky full of stars. It was just dawning on them that Arthur was safe.

Tamar stood up, her legs shaking as she walked – and then ran – towards Arthur. She very nearly knocked him off his feet as she cannoned into him, crushing him in an immense hug. Eventually she released him, wiping her cheek with her hand. It was damp and sticky; covered with Arthur's blood.

Nick was only a split second behind her. 'Mate, I thought you were going to fall right down that shaft …'

Tamar and Nick looked at one another and then back to Arthur, standing pale and exhausted with his clothes torn and blood seeping from his forehead.

'Steady, steady,' Michael instructed as he joined them. 'Time enough for all of that later.'

He looked around. 'There's some unfinished business round 'ere. You sit down, I'll be back dreckly. Fly,' he ordered, 'Stay!'

Immediately both Fly and Lightning sat down either side of the youngsters.

The three friends sat in a row, Nick to one side of Arthur and Tamar the other. She sneaked her hand into his as Bedivere moved off to Michael's side. Meanwhile Gawain waited, slightly apart from the trio, not wanting to intrude.

They watched Michael and Bedivere approach the mine building and realised that they were looking for something, or someone. The two men made for the side of the hill where Matearnas had fallen, and disappeared behind it. Arthur held his breath and watched and waited until they reappeared a few minutes later. Their expressions were grim. The Crow Man and the white hound were missing. At some point, probably when Matearnas was trying to escape, Arthur's abductor had slipped away. Michael walked back towards the young people, engaged in quiet conversation with Bedivere.

As they drew nearer Arthur stirred himself. 'The Crow Man, he's gone hasn't he?'

Michael looked at him with concern. 'Yes, he's disappeared, but I don't think we need to worry for now. I'm reckonin' he'll be taking 'iself far away from this place; t'is too dangerous for him – for the time being anyhow.'

For a while he stood with his eyes up to the night sky, listening to some internal voice. After a while he nodded.

'He's a long way from 'ere – an' he'll not be back in a hurry.'

He continued, 'There's work to be done both 'ere and at the Granite House, but it'll wait till mornin'.'

He leant down and, holding out a strong hand, helped Arthur to his feet. 'You all right now, boy?'

Arthur nodded and Michael, scrutinising his face, caught a glimpse of the iron resolve that had kept him going through the last few hours.

He smiled. 'You'll do Arthur Penhaligon – you'll do.'

Nick and Tamar heaved themselves to their feet. Lightning was ecstatic to be reunited with his adopted owner, and Arthur, feeling the touch of a wet nose on his hand, smiled for the first time that evening.

'Michael,' Tamar started hesitantly, 'what are we going to do about ...?' She gestured in the direction of Matearnas's body.

Michael had obviously already considered the options and nodded towards Arthur. 'The livin' be more important than the dead. I'll be sortin' that out later.'

And without another word, he set off and they followed, picking their way over uneven ground and clambering around boulders, until they reached a stony path. Anyone meeting them would have been puzzled by such a strange group. Especially perhaps by the horse's master who, more than ever, looked like an ancient knight and yet was in deep conversation with a modern-day boy covered in cuts and bruises.

After a while Michael slowed down and spoke quietly to Arthur. 'When we get back to the cottage you've got to be ready for the Call. Many have been waitin' and watchin' for you. They're gathering now.'

Arthur glanced at Michael and thought about everything that Matearnas and then Bedivere had said, or implied, during that long day. He still had no idea what it was all about.

Michael simply said, 'Everythin' will be made clear. Just do as Angela asks.'

Questions filled Arthur's head but before he could say anything he glimpsed a sleek shape prowling at their side.

Michael, following the direction of Arthur's look, bowed his head and smiled. 'My thanks to you, friend.'

There was a familiar, deep purr and a flick of a tail, and the creature disappeared.

'Is that what I think it is?' Nick asked, squinting into the darkness. 'Why was that woman so terrified of it?'

There was a brief silence before Michael spoke. 'T'is about what you expect to see and the side you're on. Matearnas was on the side of darkness. No harm was planned for 'er. Her own beliefs and fears were the instruments of 'er end.'

He sighed. 'T'was a waste of a life; but we all makes our own choices and she'd made 'ers many years ago. Even at the end she could 'ave changed – but there was no turnin' her.'

Arthur thought of his own brushes with the mysterious beast and caught Michael's eye, but the big man merely smiled and nodded towards the welcoming lights of the cottage.

Destiny waited.

Chapter 21

Preparations

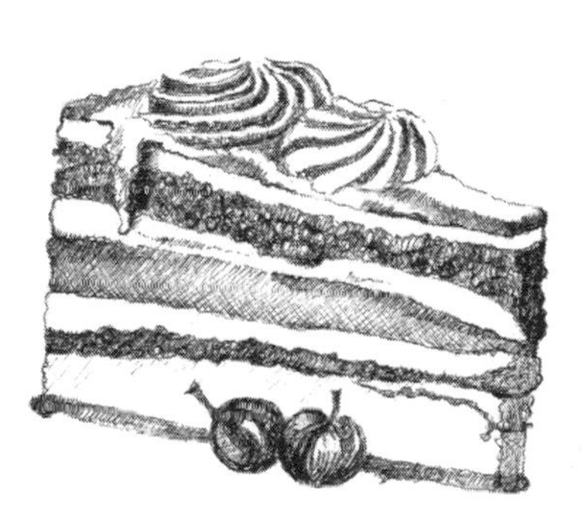

As they approached the little moorland house they noticed a couple of cars pulled up, wrenching them back to their everyday lives. One was a police car. Arthur groaned. At this rate, every policeman and woman in the county would know his name and address off by heart! The other belonged to the Penhaligons.

Arthur was mortified. He'd hardly given the outside world a passing thought. He looked at Nick and Tamar and saw their expressions – he wasn't the only one whose priorities had shifted.

'Well, it seems we 'ave company.' Michael glanced at the four youngsters. 'Angela will need to talk with you, so be ready.'

The dogs bounded ahead of them, a blur of black and white fur and wagging tails, so by the time Arthur walked through the cottage door, his dad was already on his feet. He was surprised; he'd expected to see his mum. In a corner of his mind he noticed that he had a mug of tea in his hands, and a plate of cakes in front of him. Angela had been delivering her own particular brand of reassurance.

He glanced at the grandfather clock; an angel was gesticulating and talking to another angel. This time he didn't doubt what he'd seen. Weirdly, it felt almost normal! He even managed a quick smile at them before turning his attention to his dad.

'Arthur, you've given us a scare!' he exclaimed, and wrapped his arm around Arthur's shoulders. 'Where've you been? Your mum and I have been so worried. Mum stayed at home in case you turned up there. We'll give her a ring straightaway and let her know you're safe.'

John Penhaligon stood back and took a good look at his son, reassuring himself that he was still in one piece.

Wanting to avoid his dad's scrutiny, Arthur simply said, 'I'm fine Dad, only a few cuts and bruises.' But then he glanced down and took in the state of his jeans. 'Um, but these might have had it.'

'I think we can cope with that! In the circumstances I doubt that Mum will care.' He smiled a watery smile. 'Jeans are replaceable.'

***

While Mr Penhaligon was talking to Arthur, Nick and Tamar had stopped dead in their tracks. For the first time, they too had noticed the angels – and were riveted to the spot. Michael chuckled quietly before turning to the policeman. (Fortunately he was sitting with his back to the clock.)

'What these folks need is some food and a hot drink. T'is chilly out there, even if it is summer.' And before the policeman had time to protest, Michael was addressing the youngsters. 'Why don't you all go through to the kitchen? I think Angela may be able to find you somethin' to eat.'

He looked above their heads at his sister and she, understanding his meaning, nodded.

The policeman looked surprised – he wasn't used to other people taking the initiative.

Turning back to the officer, Michael announced, 'I'll be tellin' you all I can. There will be time enough to speak to them,' he gestured towards Arthur and his friends, 'tomorrow.'

The policeman, realising he had little choice in the matter, agreed. 'That's a good idea, Mr Jolly. I'll update my colleagues and let them know that the children are safe and … is there any more of that cake?'

He looked around hopefully and, helping himself to a generous slice, settled back into the armchair as he took out his notebook and radio.

By now Nick and Tamar had just about recovered from seeing the angels and Nick was tuned into the conversation between the policeman and Michael.

He nudged Gawain. 'Think we know who's in charge around here.'

Gawain grinned and whispered, 'Yeah … not the guy in uniform.'

Tamar slid Nick a meaningful look. He was impossible. Nothing ever stopped him for long.

Meanwhile Michael had turned to Arthur's dad and was suggesting that he should phone his wife and the other parents. And Mr Penhaligon looked at the clock (with its now still angels) and exclaimed, 'Is that the time!'

But Arthur had caught the looks passing between Michael and his sister and knew that something else was going on; something far more important than making sure that they all had something to eat. He had to mobilise his friends and there was one way guaranteed to do it.

Following Angela through to the kitchen he looked over his shoulder. 'Hey guys, how about some cake?'

Nick was first through the door.

***

The kitchen was warm and inviting. A huge kitchen range took up one wall and an old farmhouse table sat squarely in the middle of the room. It was loaded with plates of cakes and a large jug of hot chocolate.

Angela cut the cake. 'Don't hold back, help yourselves.'

They didn't need a second invitation.

Angela smiled. Then she asked, 'And do you 'appen to have another man with you … someone called Bedivere?'

Puzzled, Tamar said, 'Yes we do, I think he went round to the back of the house.'

'Ah that's good. He'll be making preparations,' she said quietly – and smiled to herself.

'I don't know what he's doing,' Nick said, picking a chocolate muffin, 'but he said he won't be long.'

And sure enough, a few minutes later Bedivere let himself in through the back door and, crossing the room in a couple of strides, crushed Angela in a huge embrace. A clock ticked and, in the adjoining room, Michael could just be heard talking to the policeman and Mr Penhaligon.

Eventually, Bedivere released her and stood back. 'So many years since our last meeting.'

'Many years indeed, old friend,' Angela agreed, smoothing her skirts. 'You've 'ad a long, long time to wait.'

'So have we all!' Bedivere flicked the briefest of looks towards Arthur and the frown, which had briefly settled on his forehead, vanished. 'But the wait has not been in vain. The boy has been found.'

Tamar looked from Angela to Bedivere. She licked some cream off her fingers and asked, 'D'you two know each other then?'

Smiling, Bedivere nodded. 'I've known this fair lady for many a year.'

Tamar examined Angela. Were her eyes deceiving her or was she looking younger and was her hair changing from grey to blonde? She wondered if any of the boys had noticed but then remembered that boys don't usually spot that sort of thing.

A harp stood in one corner of the kitchen. From time to time a string moved and a single note would fill the air. It was an indication of how their world had shifted that neither Arthur nor Tamar, or even Nick, paid any attention to it. The cake was much more interesting. They were ravenous.

Angela tapped Bedivere's arm and pointed at a clock (without angels) on the dresser. 'T'is nearly time.'

'All is ready.'

'Then I'll be making our other guests comfortable,' Angela said, picking up another plate heaped with food. 'Some'ow time passes when you're warm and well-fed. And there's somethin' about that room ...'

She winked at them, leaving the words hanging in the air, and carried the plate through to the sitting room.

Bedivere started to explain. 'Tonight's work is not quite done. The most important part has been left until the last.'

He stood up and motioned towards the back door. 'Will you all come outside?'

'But we've only just got here!' Tamar exclaimed.

Bedivere replied, 'That is so ... but what you think is the end is only the beginning.'

Angela came back into the kitchen and nodded at Bedivere. Arthur, witnessing their unspoken communication, watched the old knight walk purposefully towards the back door and caught the glance Bedivere sent him. And Arthur understood. This was what Michael must have meant.

Scraping his chair back he stood up and signalled for the others to follow. Together they stepped from the warm kitchen into the cold night air. The sky was clear, studded with stars, while the full moon shone, bathing the moors in bright blue light.

Bedivere had led his now-youthful horse to the back of the cottage and was retrieving an object wrapped in rough, brown sacking from the saddle bag.

He looked at Gawain and, smiling, said, 'This is what those books in your uncle's shop speak of.'

Gawain's face was a picture as he tried to work out what Bedivere meant – and how he knew about his uncle's shop - when he broke into a huge, unbelieving grin, 'Is it real then?'

'Hey,' Nick interjected, 'what about Tamar, Arthur and me? Shouldn't we be let in on the secret? No offence Gawain, but we've all been through it today so I reckon that makes us all pretty much equal.'

Gawain glanced at Nick and, far from being offended, if anything his smile grew. In his own way, Nick had just accepted him as part of the group.

Angela nodded thoughtfully. 'True enough.'

So Bedivere started to un-wrap the package, but even before he'd finished, light was seeping through the sacking.

Gently, he withdrew the hilt of a sword.

Chapter 22

The Commissioning

The sword was magnificent. Both the hilt and the scabbard were exquisitely engraved and inlaid with precious stones. And then the air seemed to ripple, distorting Arthur's vision, so that he could see both the present and the past, as if the two were being brought together. He thought he caught a glimpse of a dark-haired stranger, maybe a few years older than him, who grinned and raised his hand in salute before disappearing.

But before he had time to digest what this could mean he was drawn back to the present by Tamar whispering, 'Look!' And she wasn't looking towards the sword but out over the moors.

There behind them, stretching into the distance, covering the moorland as far as the eye could see in the moonlight, was an immense crowd.

It was an awe-inspiring sight. Where had they all come from?

Angela explained, 'They've come in answer to the Call. As soon as you were safe it was sent out. Many have been watchin' and waitin' for this night.'

'The Call?' Arthur asked.

'To summon them – so that they may be witness to what 'as long been foretold.'

Tamar cast her eyes over the crowd and saw that Argo, the stallion, was there. Before she knew what she was doing she found herself giving him a little wave. She glanced, a little embarrassed, at the others, wondering if they'd seen; but they were too preoccupied with their own thoughts to take any notice of her. And then she was drawn back by a whinny. Argo was returning her greeting.

Arthur identified several people who, in different ways, had been instrumental in his journey: the man he'd met walking on the moors, the shopkeeper from Pendrym, and even the bus driver.

Also there, but unseen by Arthur, were the two Watchers; one with sandals on his feet and the other still wearing a street cleaner's uniform.

And the Writer was there. For once she was simply standing and waiting like the crowds around her, ready to witness what was to come.

Nor had he noticed his dad slip out of the cottage, leaving the policeman to his radio and note-taking, only to linger in the shadows while wondering at the spectacle.

But Arthur did see the pale stranger he'd last seen after he'd rescued little Kensa. He glanced at Bedivere and, from his expression, realised that he too had noted the stranger's presence. The old knight was ready with the sword in his hand, frowning and hesitating, but then he stepped forward; this act must be completed – no matter who was present.

So Arthur turned from surveying the crowd and focused on Bedivere ... and instinctively understood what had to happen next. He didn't need anyone to tell him. This was what had brought such a crowd of witnesses to this remote and ancient place.

Slowly, Arthur walked towards the knight as the sword was raised and held out towards him, and he listened to Bedivere's words, 'T'is yours, sire. I was once charged with a duty and I have lived these many years in the hope of seeing this day and now it has come. You are its rightful heir and you are justly named.'

He continued, 'But first I think you know what must be done.'

***

The air rippled again and the curtains of time were drawn back. Looking past Bedivere it was as if he was watching a trailer for a film, but Arthur knew that a moment in history was being replayed just for him. He saw a knight kneeling and the flat of a sword lightly touching each shoulder. Arthur peered at the scene being played in front of him and realised that he recognised the sword. It was the one that Bedivere was holding. Then the knight stood and, turning towards Arthur, smiled; it was the dark haired stranger he'd briefly seen on the moor.

Another ripple and the man disappeared.

***

Arthur knelt and, as the sword touched his shoulder, all his questions and worries fell away.

Everything had been leading towards this moment. He didn't understand all the events that had got them there, but he had no doubt that this was where they had been heading.

A sigh spread throughout the crowd. For many of them this was a long-awaited event, the culmination of many dreams. But for Arthur's three companions it wasn't quite as straightforward; they were just doing their best to take in the latest in a line of extraordinary events.

As the sword was lowered from his shoulder Arthur stood up and Bedivere offered him the hilt. Slipping his hand around the grip it felt as if the sword had been made for him, as if he'd always owned it.

He looked up at the old knight who nodded, smiling his understanding and approval, and then Arthur turned and advanced towards his friends.

Tamar cast a fleeting look towards Nick. Their eyes met and she raised her eyebrows in a question but he bobbed his head towards Gawain on her other side. She turned. Gawain was kneeling, as Arthur had, and finally she understood what was expected of them.

Feeling a little awkward both she and Nick followed Gawain's example. It was significant that for once Nick said nothing. Then each of them felt the flat of the sword on their shoulders, marking them out for the future.

'T'is well done, sire,' said Bedivere.

'Eh, well done indeed,' a deep voice agreed.

They hadn't noticed Michael join them but without him this wouldn't have been complete.

'Arthur, the sword must be put away for a while, to be kept safe,' Michael said gently. 'Its work is done for now. The time will come when you will be reunited, but for the present ...'

Without the need for further explanation Arthur understood and carefully, if somewhat reluctantly, handed it back to Bedivere.

'An' now it's time for the last part of the Commissioning,' Angela announced.

And immediately it felt as though they were floating in the night sky, high above the moors. High enough to be able to look down on tiny villages with their lights twinkling – and out to the wide expanses of the flat, calm sea glinting in the moonlight. Over hills to the coasts and up towards the river Tamar and down to the isles beyond Land's End. And there was a castle, ruined and alone, clinging to a rocky cliff where it stood proudly – waiting.

But who was that fleeing figure with his collar turned up and his coat flapping and a white dog at his side? Could it be the Crow Man? They were too far away to be clearly seen.

Then Angela's voice cut in. 'This is a special land and no mistake. From time to time it gives us special people.

'People whose duty and birth-right it is to care for and guard those less strong than themselves. We never know when such people are born. Usually they arrive in ones, sometimes twos, but it seems we 'ave four of you together.

'Four Guardians of our land and its people.

'So they be special times we be livin' through

'These last few days 'ave been a test for you, just the first. Only time will tell when the next will come, but always remember that the light can overcome any darkness.

'Look down now an' remember. Look at the hills an' sea, the rivers and the land and think on all that is contained within an' above it. When you are called you must all be ready.

'Ready to defend an' protect what 'as been given to you. Ready to be Guardians of all that is right.'

The words faded and they were once more standing on the soft turf outside the cottage. No one moved and not one of the four spoke as the stars glinted and an owl screeched.

But after a few moments Arthur arrived at a decision and, turning to Bedivere, asked, 'Can I have the sword back? Just for a minute?'

Without a word, Bedivere drew the sword out of its scabbard and handed it back to him.

Arthur turned to face the silent crowd.

He paused, taking in the spectacle, before raising the sword high above his head. Even those at the furthermost edges of the gathering were able to see the boy and the sword silhouetted on the hill's summit. And every one of them was able to hear the words that followed.

'We will stand together – and together we will protect this people and this land. We will stand for all that is right and for all that is true. For Cornwall. For ever!'

Arthur stood with the sword raised high above his head and felt a surge of pride and affection for this place and its people.

The words carried and echoed across the moors and out to sea. And then a whisper, as light as a breeze, passed through the crowd. The whisper grew until it became a roar of approval reverberating through the hills and valleys, from the river Tamar to the shores of the islands flung far out at Cornwall's tip.

Mr Penhaligon, keeping to the shadows of the cottage, felt tears of pride prickle his eyes and a little worm of fear tickle his insides. He was overwhelmed by the sheer *otherness* of it all – and that his son was right at the centre of this weird and wonderful event.

Who would have guessed it? he thought. *My son!*

All he wanted was to hold him close so that no harm could ever come to him, but it was clear that Arthur's life wouldn't necessarily be safe – and it certainly wasn't going to be ordinary. John Penhaligon took a deep breath, pulled out his hanky and blew his nose.

He supposed that his job was to carry on parenting in the real world ... and allow Arthur to get on with this other life. Tucking his hanky back in his pocket, he came to a decision: he would never mention this evening unless Arthur brought it up first. Only then would he admit to seeing Arthur being made a Guardian. Having decided this, he quietly slipped back into the cottage. At least he could ensure that the policeman was safely occupied with his radio and notebook.

'Well said, Arthur,' Bedivere said.

'Yeah mate, no going back now!' Nick added, as ever straight to the point. 'Don't think that guy over there is too impressed though.'

Nick nodded in the direction of the pale stranger.

Although still standing nonchalantly with his arms crossed, the pale man was staring at Arthur, for the first time making direct eye contact with him. His whole demeanour had changed from neutral to openly hostile and ice-cold. Arthur was left in no doubt that this man hated him – and everything he stood for. His elation disappeared, replaced by a dawning understanding of what might lie ahead.

'Man, he's some piece of work!' Nick murmured.

'Who is he?' Tamar asked, catching a glimpse of the stranger.

'Dunno,' Arthur replied. 'Wish I did.'

As they watched, the stranger scornfully bowed his head in Arthur's direction, then turned and vanished into the crowd.

'Boy, I wouldn't like to meet him on a dark night!' Nick said.

'Cheers Nick,' Arthur muttered.

He turned to Bedivere and realised that the old knight had witnessed all that had just happened. Arthur held up the sword for Bedivere to take.

'You saw him too, then?' Arthur asked.

'Aye, sire, I did.' Bedivere replied, taking the sword and sliding it into the scabbard. 'But don't let the ill-will of one man outweigh the goodwill of many.'

He gestured towards the open moors and to the crowd who'd been drawn together from far and wide and were now, reluctantly, starting to disperse.

Despite these reassuring words Arthur was filled with a deep foreboding. He knew that the pale stranger would appear again.

Chapter 23

The end of the beginning

But Arthur's dark thoughts were interrupted by Michael.

Tearing his gaze from the departing crowd, he saw that he and his friends were each being handed chains with miniature swords attached to them. They were exact replicas of the full-sized weapon he'd been holding only minutes before.

'These be for you to use, for your protection. You must always keep them near to you,' Michael was telling them. 'Never let them leave your side.'

Glancing down at the sword and chain, Arthur saw that the others had been given silver swords but that his was pure gold.

'Sire,' Michael said addressing him. 'You 'ave been Chosen. From the moment of your birth it was ordained for you to be the Guide; to lead those around you an' protect others yet to be shown to you.

'At times this will be a heavy burden, but remember you never 'ave to carry it alone, there will always be those ready to come to your aid.'

Arthur considered the implications of all that Michael had said. He ran the chain through his fingers. He had begun to suspect that his life would be altered in some way, but he hadn't anticipated quite so much resting on his shoulders.

He thought about the challenge of saving little Kensa from the river.

Of the Crow Man somewhere out there on the moors.

And the pale stranger.

He swallowed. The certainty and euphoria that he'd known just minutes before had deserted him. All he felt now was doubt and insecurity.

He started to speak, 'The thing is Michael, I don't feel … well, I'm not sure that I'm up to this. There must be someone who could do it better than me.'

He paused, trying to frame what he wanted to say. 'I mean, I don't think that I'm brave enough, or whatever, to take this on.'

He trailed off, unable to meet Michael's eyes and the disappointment that he felt sure he'd see there.

The breeze dropped, not a blade of grass moved. The leaves in the nearby hawthorn tree stilled. Nature held its breath – waiting. Even Bedivere's horse had edged towards the group and was standing with its gaze firmly fixed on Arthur.

'Arthur.' Bedivere's quiet voice broke into the silence. 'If ever a man considers himself worthy to lead others, then he will never be a true leader.'

Arthur looked at the old knight but before he was able to utter a word, Nick was talking. 'Mate, remember that game we used to play at school when we were little kids? You know, when we were about five?'

Arthur frowned, casting his mind back while wondering what on earth this had to do with anything. Meanwhile Gawain was looking questioningly at Tamar, who just shrugged, equally baffled.

'You know, we used to hide behind stuff in the playground and pretend it was us against the rest of the world.'

'Yeah, I remember, but I don't ...'

'And,' Nick continued, 'remember how we used to end the game?'

Arthur thought and then his face cleared. 'Oh yeah! "Together – for ever."'

'Well, that's us, isn't it mate?'

Gawain and Tamar finally understood what Nick was getting at and were nodding vigorously, agreeing.

'See?' Nick said, encompassing them with a wave of his arm. 'We're all in this together. It's not just you. It'll be like... like those muska-whatsits.'

'Musketeers,' Gawain finished for him, grinning.

'Yeah, those.'

Tamar stifled a giggle.

Arthur contemplated what was being offered and glanced towards Michael, who was watching him but saying nothing. This had to be his decision

He ran the chain through his fingers and, once again, saw Great-Uncle Lance entrusting the model of the knight into his care and heard those words.

In that instant he knew what he had to do.

He looked at Michael and nodded; he didn't need to say anything.

There was a rustle as the leaves were brushed by the lightest of breezes. Then Bedivere's horse whinnied and, high above them, the stars pulsed.

Resting his hand on Arthur's shoulder, Bedivere said, 'You will be a true Guardian, one that would make Lance proud.'

Arthur's head snapped up at the mention of his great-uncle but, before he was able to say anything, Bedivere had turned to Nick. 'And you, Nick. You spoke with honour.'

Nick, unused to such praise, especially from someone like Bedivere, shuffled uncomfortably but Angela came to his rescue by nodding meaningfully towards the cottage.

Pulled back to the other reality, they suddenly remembered that both the policeman and Arthur's dad were waiting for them inside.

'Come on guys,' Gawain said. 'They'll be wondering what's happened to us.'

Michael hurriedly gestured to the chains as they walked towards the door. 'Put them on an' remember, always keep them close.'

Nick nudged Arthur. 'Hey mate, I never thought I'd wear something like this. Bling isn't my thing!'

Arthur grinned. His friend had a way of bringing him back to earth. 'Might be an idea to put it inside your shirt then Nick, otherwise everyone'll want one.'

They wandered towards the cottage but Arthur dropped behind. He turned back to Bedivere who was preparing his horse, getting ready to leave.

'Will we meet again?'

'Ah, sire, that's something beyond my say. I know not what lies in the future.'

Arthur held out his hand to Bedivere. The old knight clasped it warmly.

'I hope we do, though.'

'Aye, sire. But always remember that when you need this,' he said, gesturing to the sword now safely stowed away and hanging at his side on the saddle, 'it will be waiting.'

Arthur wondered when that would be. Reluctantly he looked over his shoulder towards the open door of the cottage.

'I've got to go; they'll be waiting for me.'

Bedivere nodded and regarded Arthur silently. Then, in a single, fluid movement he was on his horse and turning it towards the wide open spaces of the moor.

'Give my farewell to the others Arthur, and may courage go with you.'

With that he raised his hand in a final salute, gave the signal to his mount and was off, his hair and cloak flying out, carrying his precious cargo to its hiding place.

***

Arthur approached the back door of the cottage deep in thought. Michael was waiting for him, leaning against the door frame.

'He's gone,' Arthur said.

Michael nodded. 'There's work still to be done.'

Both man and boy were silent, thinking over all that had happened and maybe what was yet to come.

Arthur stirred himself, for the first time taking in the scene before him. Nick was eating what was left of the cakes while Tamar and Gawain chatted – as if they'd known one another all their lives and they'd had a perfectly ordinary evening.

He glanced at his watch. 'Better get this show on the road. Come on guys.'

'Hey,' replied Nick with a mouthful of cake, 'we were waiting for you, your sire-ship.'

'Nick!' Tamar exclaimed, thumping his arm.

'What?'

'Oh, never mind.' she said, getting up. 'Come on Gawain, race you to the car.'

Immediately both Nick and Gawain shoved their chairs back and made a dash for the door, shouting for Arthur to follow.

There was so much more that Arthur wanted to ask. He turned towards Michael, hesitating.

But Michael rested his hand on Arthur's shoulder. 'You did well today. You'll do well in the future – and don't forget – you will never 'ave to work alone. You'll always 'ave the …' he paused and broke into a broad grin, his eyes twinkling, 'other musketeers to help you!'

He stood back. 'They'll be waiting for you – your sireship.'

'I know, I just wish …'

'This world's full of unanswered questions, Arthur. But it's also full of adventure and wonder. An' I'm reckonin' that you and the other Guardians are goin' to see a fair amount of both; so don't worry about the questions. Just enjoy the journey and the answers – when you find them.'

A shout summoned Arthur; his time with Michael was up. He would have to wait to find out more. Arthur looked at his new, old friend and for the second time in one evening, held out his hand to say a reluctant goodbye.

'We'll meet again, Arthur,' his friend said, although he didn't say when that would be.

The cat strolled in, fixed the boy with its green eyes and walked past. Arthur didn't notice its fur switching from ginger to black, or its paws expand and contract, before settling on being the paws of a small cat again.

Arthur followed his friends through the empty sitting room. The grandfather clock ticked. He caught a movement out of the corner of his eye and saw the angels in the clock dancing and bowing. He smiled and bowed in return, wondering about this world which danced alongside his own, fusing and blending with normal life.

As he stepped outside the cottage a barn owl swooped overhead and, a little way off, he heard a deep, rumbling purr.

***

And now …

The Writer sits at her desk, the candles flickering. She regards the moonlit street, and a large, ginger cat appears, prowling towards her garden. It leaps onto the wall and sits and waits.

Minutes later two men stroll along Castle Close, one is pushing a cart. They are talking, their heads inclined to one another. Eventually they draw level with the house and face the window … and bow.

The Writer nods an acknowledgement, and a feather pen dips itself into a glass pot of gold ink, flies into her hand and Writes. The first part of the story is complete.

***

Across town, in Nick's kitchen, a book turns its pages until it comes to an illustration. If there was anyone to look at it they would see that it is a picture of a boy.

The boy isn't alone.

He is standing at the edge of a lake on a windswept moor, being watched by a woman seated on a horse.

And in the centre of the lake a hand is rising out of the water – holding a sword … but that's another story.

Dear Reader,

I hope that you enjoyed reading *The Golden Sword* as much as I enjoyed writing and illustrating it.

If you liked it, I would be delighted and honoured if you could post a rating or review on Amazon and Goodreads. It would make my day.

At the very end of the book, I've included places where you can contact me. I always love hearing from my readers.

Thank you,
Rosie

The Time Smugglers

Chapter 1

The enemy returns

The seal pushed himself off the rocks and slid into the sea.

Moments later he emerged beneath the creaking hull of the ship, its masts swaying with the rise and fall of the water. The animal swam from stern to bow before coming to rest below the prow.

Above the seal, a figure leant over the rail, surveying the cliffs rising from the water's edge. His gaze was drawn towards a tiny hamlet nestling in a wooded valley.

A light flickered in a cottage window; a door opened and snatches of conversation escaped into the night. The man leant further forward, straining to catch the words, but was interrupted by a shout from somewhere deep inside the ship. He turned, irritated, and after casting a quick look back towards the cottage disappeared from his watch. Below him, the sea-hidden spy vanished beneath the waves as silently as he'd arrived.

The Guardians' enemies were gathering.

***

'Are you staying with your aunt all summer?' Tamar asked.

'Dunno, depends how long Mum and Dad are away I suppose,' Arthur replied.

'Well, it's a pretty cool place to stay,' Nick said. 'It's great having the beach at the end of the garden.'

Arthur, watching a vapour trail stretch across the wide blue sky, nodded, agreeing. The three of them were sitting on a hillside above a secluded bay with fields and woods running down to the sea. Sheep dotted the steep, green land behind them and a tractor chugged along the brow of the hill. Arthur knew that it was almost ideal, and it would have been if it weren't for that prickle of apprehension stubbornly lodged between his shoulder blades.

Although they were unaware of it, they made an interesting trio, with Tamar and her waist-length curtain of black hair, and the two boys, one blond and the other dark haired. However his appearance, or anyone else's, was the last thing on Arthur's mind. He was sure that something was wrong.

He gazed at the view – and wondered.

'Is Gawain coming over?' Tamar asked. 'I thought you said that he'd be here.'

'Yeah,' Nick agreed, 'when I spoke to him he told me that he was going to have time off today.'

But Arthur was temporarily distracted by a movement on the beach below them. 'What?'

Squinting into the sun, he narrowed his eyes and focused on the rocks rearing up at the edge of the beach. He thought that he'd glimpsed a familiar figure disappear behind them moments before.

'Gawain,' Nick repeated, 'he should be here.'

'Oh ... yeah,' Arthur replied, watching the rocks. He had a feeling that the person had been wearing a long coat and a wide-brimmed hat; the preferred clothing of the Crow Man. But as fast as the idea took shape he banished it. Surely there was no way that his old enemy could be here, in Porth Talant?

'Arthur!' Tamar exclaimed impatiently. 'You're not listening to a word we're saying!'

He pulled himself back. 'Oh right, Gawain ... no, he can't come over. He's helping in his uncle's shop.'

Gawain was the fourth of the Guardians. In the last year they'd spent a lot of time together. After all, nobody else would understand the strange world they'd entered when they'd been made Cornwall's Guardians. They really had become the four musketeers, as Nick had called them, bonded by magic and duty. It wasn't that they consciously tried to exclude other people – it was just easier when it was the four of them. And it felt safer.

'That's tough, I bet he's fed up.' Nick fiddled with a tiny, silver sword hanging from a chain around his neck, but already his grasshopper mind had moved on. 'Do you guys still keep your swords on all the time?'

Tamar nodded as she toyed with the sword and chain that she'd been given. 'I do.'

Arthur tore his gaze away from the rocks. 'Of course … Michael told us we *had* to wear them all the time.'

'Yeah,' Nick said, 'but we don't really know what they're for, and it's been a whole year since we saw him.' He paused. 'Everything's been so normal, I'm beginning to wonder if anything interesting will ever happen!'

They thought about that night a year ago; its magic and their commissioning. But Nick was right. Nothing even slightly unusual had happened since then.

Together they contemplated the view laid out in front of them: a seagull idly drifting high above the bay; cotton-wool clouds dotting the blue sky and waves lapping the soft, Cornish sand. Looking at all of this it was hard to believe that anything *could* happen.

Arthur stretched and stroked Lightning, his constant canine companion of the last year, and looked at the hill behind him. He watched the tractor slow as it approached the gate and saw the farmer jump down to open it. He was so absorbed, wondering whether it was Farmer Martin or one of his sons, that he didn't notice the long-limbed figure reappear and scramble over the rocks at the edge of the beach – accompanied by a midnight-feathered bird. Neither did he see the man pick up a piece of driftwood lying on the sand and weigh it thoughtfully in his hand, before disappearing behind a rocky outcrop.

In the bay below them a sun-hatted toddler was busy examining a rock pool and further out to sea yachts glided, while towards the shore people swam and paddled. It was a picture-perfect scene.

But an instant later their peace was shattered by Tamar grabbing the chain hanging around her neck and almost yelling, 'Ow, my sword – it's *freezing*!'

'So's mine!' Nick exclaimed.

'And mine.' Arthur grasped his chain, swinging the sword away from his neck.

They looked at one another. This had to be more than just a coincidence.

And Arthur was reminded of the stones left for him by the Crow Man the previous year – because they'd done this too. Whenever anything, or anyone, dangerous had been nearby the stones had reacted, their temperature dropping just like this.

He looked down to the beach and up to the hills but he couldn't see or hear anything different; the tractor was still there and the children were still playing on the sand, but he'd learnt that appearances could be deceptive. It looked like the waiting that Nick had been complaining about might be finally over.

'Be careful what you wish for!' he muttered.

And suddenly Lightning sat bolt upright.

'Can you feel it too?' Arthur asked his dog.

It was obvious that something had grabbed the dog's attention because he was standing, every muscle tensed, concentrating on the beach at a point where the cliff jutted out separating this bay from its neighbour. The only way of getting to the other bay was over the jagged rocks. However, before Arthur could stop him, Lightning had taken off.

'Lightning!'

But the dog was deaf to his call and was already at the base of the cliff, slithering and sliding over the treacherous rocks, determined to reach the neighbouring bay.

'Lightning, come back!'

For a split second Arthur stood undecided as to whether to follow, but this was so out of character that he knew something was wrong.

'Come on!' he yelled, and soon all three were racing down the hill towards the beach. None of them had time to see a dark bird, high in the sky above them, or a pair of black eyes surveying their progress from the water at the edge of the rocks.

But they all heard the barking, the yelp, and the sudden silence.

***

They scrabbled around the base of the cliff, splashing through rock pools and over slimy seaweed. Rounding the corner, they slid down the rocks to the deserted beach and Arthur's stomach flipped. A black and white shape lay at the water's edge. Blood was seeping from the body, staining the sand rose-pink and running in tiny rivulets to mingle with the sea.

'Lightning!' Arthur's shout echoed off the surrounding cliffs.

He rushed to where the dog lay and leant over to stroke him but there was no reaction. Frantically he searched the animal's body. His hand travelled over Lightning's silky back and up towards his head to find blood bubbling from a deep gash in the dog's skull.

Nick and Tamar were just behind Arthur but it took a few moments before the realisation hit them that the limp form on the sand was Arthur's dog.

They looked on, shocked, as Arthur talked to Lightning, willing him to move and oblivious to the waves inching their way up the beach as the tide hurried in.

'Who did this to you?' Arthur murmured as he stroked Lightning's still body. He felt sick as a dull dread began to take hold. Mesmerised, he watched beads of blood flowing from the open wound, and listened to Lightning's breathing becoming lighter. Tears misted his vision. He couldn't believe that this dog, which barely ever left his side, was dying in front of him. That there was nothing he could do to save him.

However the tide wouldn't stop for anyone. The water was creeping in, crawling up the beach and starting to lap around Nick's feet. Arthur's friend glanced up from watching Lightning to find the sea edging up the sand. It would only take a few more minutes for them to be completely stranded. There was no way out of the bay other than over the rocks – and soon they'd be submerged. They had to get out before they were trapped.

'Arthur,' Nick said quietly. 'The tide's coming in.'

Tamar looked at the fast-rising water and understood what Nick was talking about but she shook her head. She knew that there was no way that Arthur would leave Lightning – and she wasn't about to give up on him either.

'There must be someone who can help,' she said desperately, and then a thought struck her. 'I know! Hang on a minute …' and rummaging in her bag she pulled out her phone.

'You can't get a signal down here,' Nick stated, pointing to the cliffs high above them.

Tamar's face fell. 'Oh! I'd forgotten that.'

She twisted her hair through her fingers as she thought and then her face lit up. Reaching into her bag, she pulled out her towel and thrust one end at Nick. 'We can roll him onto this, it's easily big enough, and then we can take him back.'

'There's no way we can carry him over those rocks,' Nick protested. 'They're slippery and he's a big dog. He'll be too heavy.'

Holding her end of the towel, she nodded towards Arthur. 'Come on Nick, we've *got* to try.'

Nick looked at their friend and at the incoming water. Tamar was right, it was their only option.

'Okay,' he sighed. 'Come on then, we'll give it a go.'

Arthur looked up as Nick and Tamar advanced, and understood what his friends were doing, but in his heart he knew that they were fighting against the odds. Lightning was slipping away in front of his eyes. However, he continued talking quietly to his dog, willing him to hang on long enough to get him to someone who could help. Tamar tucked the top end of the towel under Lightning's head, positioning it so that it could be pulled under his body, while Nick and Arthur stood either side, ready to lift him.

They were so caught up in their efforts that none of them noticed the prow of a rowing boat nudge into view around the rocks until a voice startled them.

'Could you be doin' with some help?'

Sitting in the boat a little way off the shore was a fisherman, his navy-blue sailing cap pushed to the back of his head and his shirt sleeves rolled up. He was leaning forward, resting on his oars, casually dipping one into the water whenever he needed to maintain the boat's position.

'You got trouble with your dog, boy?' he asked Arthur.

Arthur nodded. He couldn't bring himself to speak.

The fisherman looked around, casting his eyes over the cliffs and the woods above them, before rowing the boat further in and stepping over the side. Without a word he handed Nick a rope tethered to the boat's prow and bent down beside Lightning's body, then he gently ran his hands over the animal's head and side.

He grunted, ''e be in a bad way, but he's not done for.'

And then in one deft movement he was gathering the dog in his arms, lifting him over the side of the boat and setting him gently down on the boards. 'Come on,' he said to Arthur and his friends. 'In you get.'

Arthur snapped out of his reverie and scrambled after the fisherman. He sat on the boards of the boat cradling Lightning's head in his lap, while Tamar and Nick grabbed their bags and hurried after him. The minute they were on board the fisherman pushed the boat away from the shore and started rowing. Once they were further out he looked up at the tree-screened cliffs and frowned.

High on the cliff path, a crow flapped lazily above a man wearing a long, dark coat and a wide-brimmed hat. He was observing the progress of the little boat and making no effort to hide; in fact it was almost as if he was waiting to be seen.

And indeed, the moment that he caught the fisherman's eye he lifted up a thick branch to show him something glistening on the end of the wood. Slowly, and very deliberately, the man drew his finger along it and held it up for the fisherman to see. The end of his finger was scarlet, the colour of blood, Lightning's blood. The fisherman's face darkened and his frown deepened, but he said nothing to his passengers as the man on the cliff raised his hat and turned away.

***

Above the bay a sudden breeze swept up a pile of dead leaves and set the flowers in the hedges trembling. A second later two figures stepped out of the shadows, glanced at one another and then at the scene in front of them. Both men were slightly blurred at the edges, just a little out of focus, because both of them had been pulled from other centuries and places.

They were the Watchers, travellers in time, and they'd been summoned to Cornwall to observe Arthur and the other Guardians. They'd arrived at the moment that the fisherman had become the unwilling witness to the method of Lightning's injury. They too had seen the bloodied branch.

One said, 'So the Crow Man has arrived and already he has drawn blood!'

His companion nodded grimly. 'He will be wanting revenge, Servo.'

'Revenge? But for what?'

'For the death of Matearnas.'

'Ah, of course, the self-proclaimed Queen of Cornwall.'

Viatoris nodded. 'Sadly, the Crow Man – Brane – persists in blaming young Arthur for her death.'

The Watchers continued to study the activity below them; the man on the cliff path and the fisherman rowing his passengers and the brutally injured dog to safety.

'The Rule states that we must never intervene,' one of the Watchers said, 'but at times it is a hard command to follow.'

They were quiet as they contemplated their commission: to observe the progress of those assigned to them – but never to interfere.

His companion nodded, sighing. 'So, Servo, you have come from Watching your other charge in Egypt?'

'I have, Viatoris. He does well. And you?'

'Ah, I have been given an assignment in Italy,' the Watcher was on the point of going into more detail when a movement out at sea stopped him.

A sailing ship had appeared from behind a small island that lay a mile or two out from the mainland.

It was a magnificent vessel, fully rigged and moving smoothly across the water, which wouldn't have been particularly unusual except for the complete lack of even the smallest breeze. The wind that had earlier powered the yachts in the bay had dropped leaving the air still and heavy, yet the ship's many sails still billowed.

Viatoris plunged his hand into his shirt pocket and pulled out a velvet drawstring bag. Then he extracted a small, leather case, pressed the clasp, took out a compass and pointed it out to sea.

The face of the compass was constructed differently to most others in that there was an inner, solid circle with an ornate needle at its centre, surrounded by a separate ring which could move independently. Together the Watchers studied it as the needle came to life.

The outer ring of the compass was decorated with intricate pictures. On one side brightly painted butterflies and miniscule birds flew above exotic flowers, while on the opposite edge grey and black flowers grew and withered.

Viatoris tilted the compass and the needle wobbled and spun until it was pointing at the tall-masted ship as it sailed across the bay. Then the outer circle of the compass began to rotate.

The Watchers waited as the decorated ring made a few rotations before finally slowing to a halt to leave the needle pointing towards the ship while resting on a black and dying flower.

It appeared that the device was severely affected by its findings because the glass of the compass had started to mist over and the needle had begun to quiver.

'It is rare for her to react like this. Look, how she trembles!' said Viatoris.

They watched as the needle rocked and shook.

The owner of the compass shook his head and pulled the hand-stitched leather case out of his pocket.

With infinite care he opened the lid, placed the device inside and clicked the gold clasp shut. Then he pushed the case into the velvet pouch and tucked it into his shirt pocket, close to his chest. 'So their enemies are assembling.'

The sailing ship continued on its voyage across the bay, eventually disappearing behind the finger of land that separated Porth Talant from its neighbouring village.

The Watchers turned their attention to the little rowing boat edging around the rocks below them with its precious cargo on board, and followed it as its owner steered it towards Porth Talant. It wasn't many minutes before it too, had disappeared from their view.

Once it had gone both Watchers relaxed, certain that their charges would be safe, for now. Then Servo, dressed as a keen walker, complete with woolly hat and walking boots, turned to Viatoris. He looked him up and down, taking in his companion's cloak and shoes which looked suspiciously like those of a court jester, and started to smile.

But before he could make a comment, Viatoris said, 'I have come from Watching the young Leonardo da Vinci in Italy, five hundred years from here. The fashion of that time demands this ridiculous footwear.'

He hauled a bag out from the bushes with a flourish. 'But I am prepared!' And with that he proceeded to pull out a cap, a stripy pullover and a pair of scruffy jeans. He had the air of an 'A' class student. In anyone else it would be described as smug. But his smile faded as he searched deep inside the bag because his disguise as a fisherman was incomplete; he'd forgotten the boots. He contemplated his footwear. There was no way a Cornish fisherman would be seen dead in them. He sighed. They'd just have to do.

In an attempt to divert attention from himself, he asked, 'So you still Watch Joseph, the Dreamer, in Egypt?'

Servo, the 'walker' nodded, and was about to say something, when the wooden masted ship with its sails swollen by the non-existent wind, sailed back into view. This mission promised to be one of their more demanding projects. Overhead a dark-feathered bird circled. The men exchanged glances and picked up their bags before making their way along the cliff path.

There was Watching to be done.

***

Tamar scrutinised their rescuer as he steered the little boat around the rocks.

They'd never met but there was something familiar about him. She wondered where he lived – and how he'd managed to appear at just the right moment.

As if he'd heard her thoughts, he stated, 'I live in Porth Pyra, near your sister. My name's Jago Jolliff.'

Tamar frowned. How did he know about Morwenna, and that she was her sister?

He rowed, glancing at the cliffs and out to sea, and answered her unspoken question. 'Is there anyone in Porth Pyra who doesn't know Wenna?' The fisherman smiled. 'We're on the same side, lass.'

Tamar looked at him sharply, wondering just how much he knew.

Again, without her saying a word, he said, 'An' young Arthur's staying in Porth Talant with his Aunt Dywana.'

For once Tamar was speechless. As fast as she thought something, this man answered it, but at that moment her attention was diverted by a movement on the cliff path.

Two men, engaged in deep conversation, were walking side by side but as she watched they appeared to fade and melt into the shadows. Tamar leant forward, straining to get a better view, but they'd gone. She looked along the path – there was no sign of either man which was strange because she didn't know that there was another way off the cliff.

***

Nick, sorting their belongings, wasn't listening to the conversation. He'd found a scrap of material which he'd picked up with Tamar's towel, it looked as though it could have been torn from a coat or something. Glancing towards Arthur and Lightning, he saw a tiny fragment of the same material at the corner of Lightning's mouth and an idea began to take shape.

As they rounded the rocks edging the bay of Porth Talant, a short, round figure was running down the beach towards them with her skirts flapping. 'I've called the vet!' she was shouting. ''E'll be here dreckly.'

Tamar and Nick looked at each other. How had Dywana known they'd need a vet?

Their rescuer, catching their puzzled glances, merely said, 'Not all of us need phones to call for help.'

He gave another pull on the oars, pushing the boat onto the beach. 'For some there's more direct means.'

He gently picked up the unconscious dog and stepped over the side of the boat.

'Come on boy,' he called to Arthur. 'Let's be making your dog comfortable afore the vet gets 'ere. You two all right to pull the boat up?'

Arthur clambered out and jogged after their rescuer. Lightning's survival was the only thing on his mind.

Nick and Tamar watched them make their way up the beach before working together to pull the boat onto the sand and out of the water.

Eventually Tamar turned to Nick. 'What d'you think he meant about there being more direct means?'

'No idea,' Nick said, shrugging. 'It's the sort of thing that Michael would have said, and I didn't always understand him! Come on, I want to see how Lightning's doing.'

They walked up the beach, so preoccupied with all that had happened that neither of them noted a large ginger cat sitting on a stone wall, quietly observing them. Nor did they see it jump off the wall, its fur rippling from ginger to black and back to ginger again, as it followed them along the lane to Dywana's cottage. Cathe was back.

Thanks and notes

My thanks to Sigma Press, for their kind permission to reference Craig Weatherhill's book, *Cornish Place Names and Languages*.

Special thanks must go to Sally Vince, my ever-patient and talented editor. Every writer should have someone gifted with Sally's flair and sensitivity to guide them.

And my family have been amazing in their support and encouragement. Thank you all so much. We all need people to believe in us.

Thank you also to those friends who have helped me. You know who you are.

But most of all to Peter, my legendary, guitar-playing, science-teacher husband – this wouldn't have been finished without you.

And always – grâce à Dieu.

If you'd like to visit some of the places that inspired me, come to Cornwall. Visit Bodmin Moor and the standing stones known as King Arthur's Hall (always respect the fences around the mine shafts), and take the train along the river between Liskeard and Looe.

For photo galleries related to the books visit: http://rosie-morgan-cornwall.blogspot.co.uk

My Facebook page is: www.facebook.com/writingrosie

Goodreads at: www.goodreads.com/rosiemorgan

Cornish words

Brane = crow
Cathe = cat
Clowas, convethas = hear, understand
Hagarawall = storm
Kernow = Cornwall
Matearnas = Queen
Me ore hedna per thaa. Voyd alebma! = I know that very well. Go away!
'Proper job' – something that's been done well
'Dreckly' – something that will get done – eventually

Servo – (Latin) to watch over or observe
Viatoris – (Latin) traveller